Second Chance
SANTA

By JJ Knight
USA Today bestselling author of

Big Pickle
Hot Pickle
Spicy Pickle
Tasty Mango
Single Dad on Top
Single Dad Plus One
The Accidental Harem
Uncaged Love Series
Fight for Her Series
Reckless Attraction

Want to make sure you don't miss a release?
Join JJ's email or text list.

ABOUT SECOND CHANCE SANTA

★★★★★

Santa for the holidays? Yes, please! JJ's Knight's SECOND CHANCE SANTA is an absolutely delightful (and seriously steamy!) holiday rom com that will have you wanting your very own Mack under the tree!

~ *New York Times* bestselling author J. Kenner

★★★★★

This endearing romance is the funny, feel-good romance of the holiday season you've been looking for, where nice girls get their naughty happily ever after.

~ *USA Today* bestselling author Blair Babylon

★★★★★

JJ has done it again! She's written a Holiday Romance that is both laugh out loud and heartwarming. Be warned though, it will forever change the way you look at your mall Santa.

~ *USA Today* bestselling author Olivia Rigal

★★★ SECOND CHANCE SANTA ★★★

I never thought the love of my life would turn out to be
— a mall Santa.

What has happened to Mack McAllister?

We were law school rivals.

Absolutely insane in bed.

Our two-year fling ended when we graduated.

He had his ambitions. I had mine.

We were going to slay the competition.

Now he's sleighing it?

When I stalk him at Riverside Mall, he looks like Santa
in every way. White beard. Rosy cheeks. Kid on his
knee.

But I know better. That bowl full of jelly is hiding
ripped abs.

I've been inside that suit.

Something's happened to the Mack I knew ten years ago.

I don't know how he feels about me now, but there's only one way to find out.

Get in there and jingle those bells.

Second Chance Santa is a holiday romantic comedy about the one who got away, the perils of resting Grinch face, and all the delicious ways to unwrap a candy cane.

Edition 1.1

Casey Shay Press
PO Box 160116
Austin, TX 78716
www.jjknight.com

Paperback ISBN: 9781938150944

Cover Design: Lori Jackson
Cover Image: Wander Aguiar

1

RORY

24 Days to Christmas

I admit it. I look suspicious.

Of course I do. I'm a grown woman in a Santa line.

Alone.

Wearing a straw hat and sunglasses.

But I can't let Santa figure out who I am.

Several kids stare. Two mothers keep glancing my way and whispering. A lanky teen boy in an elf costume eyeballs me as if I'm a creeper after Santa's cache of candy canes.

Or, I suppose, Santa's *personal* candy cane.

He might be right.

But first, I have to get close enough to Santa to know.

It's been more than ten years since we laid eyes on each other, but he'd recognize me. Just as I know him, despite the red suit and white beard. I'm not fooled by that bowl full of jelly. This Santa is ripped underneath that pillow.

I've been inside that suit.

He's Mack McAllister. Or Mack Squared, as he was known when we were in law school together.

He was the roughest, toughest, most ambitious of us all. Everyone expected him to take on the world. And win.

But now he's a mall Santa?

I have to see this for myself.

I shift closer to a mother with a wiggly pile of children, hoping people will assume one of them is mine. Preferably not the one picking his nose.

This isn't quite enough to throw off the attention I'm getting. I need them to stop staring so I stay with the line until we're closer to the front. I want to take a look in Mack's eyes and see if I can read them like I once could.

Is he down on his luck? Burned out? Gone soft?

The line is slow. I need a decoy to buy me some time, so I kneel next to the nose picker, whose shoe is untied.

"Can I tie that for you?" I ask softly, shifting the sunglasses to the top of my hat now that I'm out of sight.

The mop-headed kid, probably about three, is busy bobbing a sucker in and out of his mouth, but he sticks his foot out. I balance precariously in my pencil skirt and heels, realizing my outfit isn't helping my camouflage. A power suit does not blend in here. This is the land of jeans and Lululemon. I should have changed clothes prior to my expedition.

But scoping out Santa was a last-minute decision. I was idly clicking through a lawyer networking site when I got an update notification about one of my contacts. I sucked in a breath when I saw it. Mack McAllister had taken a side gig as a Santa in a mall on the outskirts of L.A., a half-hour from my office.

I immediately dialed the mall's information desk to ask when the devastatingly handsome, rock-jawed Santa with magic fingers and a panty-melting drawl would be in the chair.

Okay, maybe I left some of those details out.

But the woman on the line knew exactly who I was talking about. "Oh, he's very popular. He'll be here today from one to six."

I set down the phone. My next meeting wasn't until four. I had time.

I told my assistant I was stepping out and raced across town, hoping that visiting Santa on a Thursday afternoon might be easier than a weekend.

I was wrong.

The line stretches around the Christmas train, designed to squeeze more dollars out of the stressed-out mothers. They are promising rides right and left if only their precious darlings will behave for a photo.

The kids are in two camps. Half of them eagerly await their shot at convincing the big guy to bring them what they want. They bounce from foot to foot, counting how many kids are in front of them and practicing their pitches.

Then there are the others. Watching kids get abandoned on the lap of a stranger in a red suit sends them into hysterics. They cry. They beg. They cling to their mothers. One or two have tried to make a run for it, only to be reeled in like oversized flounder via the leashes attached to their tiny backpacks.

My little guy is too short to see his future, so he's fairly chill. I finish the shoelace. The mother hasn't noticed I assisted one of her brood. The kid decides I'm all right and holds out his red sucker to offer me a lick.

"That's sweet," I tell him. "No, thank you."

But this sticky-fingered Romeo doesn't take no for an answer. He thrusts it at me again, and my peripheral vision tells me the mothers next to us think it's adorable.

"Thank you, sweetie," I say, hoping that sounds appropriately motherly. "It's all yours."

But the child squeezes his eyes shut. He shoves the sucker at me again, and his wail rises to a terrible pitch.

The mother whips her head around. "What are you doing to my Teddy?"

I stand straight up. "He just wanted—"

Another woman interrupts me. "That's not your kid? Why were you tying his shoe?"

The mother grabs Teddy by the back of his red overalls and drags him closer to her. "Are you a child snatcher?"

"What? No?" Panic rises in me in a way I haven't felt in years.

"Where is *your* kid?" another woman asks.

Uh oh. "I'm shopping," I say, backing away. Time to go.

I bump into the divider that separates the line from the mall traffic. I try to lift my leg to hop over the velvet rope, but of course, my skirt is too narrow. I teeter, my arms flailing.

"Stop her!" someone shouts. "She tried to kidnap one of the kids!"

The noise crescendos. Mothers yell. Children cry. Two elves rush my way.

I twist and fall on my butt, my shoe flying off. I crunch onto my bag and know I've most certainly cracked my cell phone. This stupid impulse I had keeps getting better and better.

The elves arrive, followed closely by a mall cop in a khaki uniform. He booms, "What's going on here?"

"I fell," I say, disentangling myself from the fallen divider with as much grace as I can muster. It's important in this moment to stick to the facts. "I didn't see the rope."

The mother has Teddy in her arms. "She tried to snatch my baby!"

The security guard stares down at me with a frown. "Really? Her?"

"She—she tied his shoelace!" the other woman cries, then seems to realize how crazy that sounds and steps back to melt into the line.

I manage to scramble to my feet and locate my shoe. I slip it on as I slide my bag up my shoulder. "I did help the child tie his shoe."

"That's all?" the guard asks.

"That's all," I say firmly. If this tone works on belligerent CEOs, surely it will work on a mall cop.

An elf hands me my sunglasses, which flew off when I fell. One of the lenses is missing.

"Thank you," I tell him, and tuck them into my purse. I take off the big hat and smooth my hair.

"Are you all right?" the guard asks.

I nod. "Just a little embarrassed."

The crowd hangs back, other than Teddy's mother. "What are you going to do about her? She tried to snatch my baby!" But the tone has shifted. Now she's the one who is hard to believe.

"I'm sorry. I thought he needed help." I'm in court-room mode. "I have six nieces and nephews. There's always a loose shoelace among them."

This is a lie. I'm an only child.

But the mother backs off, now uncertain about her judgment of me.

"He's adorable," I add. "Reminds me so much of sweet Charlie. He's three. Yours is close to that, right?" I pray I'm in the ballpark.

The mother frowns, clutching the boy as the elves set the rope back in place. "Three and a half."

"Such a precious age," I say.

"So everything's okay?" the guard asks. "Are we good?"

"We're good," I say.

The mother slides into her spot in the line, gathering her children close to her. It's over.

Whew.

Clearly, my recon here is done. For good. These elves know me. The guard, too. I can't come back.

Serves me right. I chose my path with Mack a decade ago. So did he. We can't go back on it now.

But I'm not entirely off the hook. As I turn around to head for the exit, I run smack into a red velvet coat.

I take my time looking up. He's as tall as he ever was. And those green eyes stare into mine with a hint of amusement.

"Rory Sheffield," he says, and the sound of my name on his lips makes me melt inside, just like it always did. "What trouble are you stirring up now?"

Well, damn. He really *does* know who's been bad or good.

2

MACK

Rory Sheffield, in the flesh.

She stands in front of me, backed by a long line of harried mothers and their little ones. It's not time for a break, and my handler protested me leaving the chair despite the commotion.

But when I realized who had caused the ruckus, I simply had to ask the next family to wait so I could check out this unexpected turn of events for myself.

Rory Ann Marie Sheffield. First in our class—she narrowly beat me out. The most studious, wildly ambitious law student in our year.

I never knew her looking like this—a tailored suit the color of champagne, gold jewelry, and a bag that costs more than most people's rent. Her hair is disheveled after the tumble she took, but otherwise you wouldn't know she hadn't just left a stylist.

For a moment I flash with other images of her. Gripping a mug of coffee early in the morning, her hair a tousled snarl that somehow made her look even sexier. Laughing on the steps of the student union, sitting among her friends, most of them in knit hats and fake leather jackets, which were all the rage at the time.

Lying below me, naked, her legs wrapped around my waist—

"Mack," she says, trying to stand taller.

I shake off the memories. "It's *Santa* in these parts."

She glances behind her. The children are all at the rope, starry-eyed because I've stepped away from my photo set. They watch my every move, some of them waving and shouting my name.

This gig is wild. I love it. Every damn bit of it.

Except maybe the nervous pee. It happens a lot more than you'd think.

"Funny seeing you here," she says.

"I could say the same." I spot a sunglass lens near her feet and bend down to scoop it up. "Yours?" I ask.

She takes it from me and stuffs it in her bag. "Thank you."

"Too bright in the mall?" I'm teasing her, and she knows it. But I enjoy the small niggle of discomfort I can see. Rory was always a tough nut to crack. And I spy a chink in her armor.

The elves and the security guard stand too close to say much, not to mention the waiting line. But I do want to know how she got here. Last I heard, she was in Boston.

"Doing some shopping?" I ask.

"It's that time of year," she says.

I wait for her to say more, but she's been trained. She knows how to avoid incriminating herself.

"Were you in line?" I ask.

Her gaze bores into me like the Grinch himself. Now that's the woman I remember. "So you're a Santa? Sports agenting wasn't enough?"

The classic redirect. Answer a question with a new question.

But I get it now. She's here to snoop.

"Doing my part to make the world a better place," I tell her, but she's not buying it. I can see it in how her eyes narrow, like she's got a lie detector built right into her retinas.

"Mack Squared, making the world a better place. Better for the million-dollar sports figures who need to make a million dollars more?"

That's a weak potshot, so I give her one right back. "Or getting guilty corporations out of nasty public relations nightmares?" The kids behind her have quieted. I give a loud "Ho, ho, ho!" for good measure.

The kids cheer.

Rory rolls her eyes. "I had to see it for myself."

"So you *are* here for me."

She doesn't give an inch. Her tone is tough as she says, "It's been a long time." She pokes my belly pillow. "You've gone soft."

"Maybe I've had a lot of milk and cookies lately."

She shakes her head. "I never thought I'd see you like this."

My internal clock tells me it's time to get back to my

red sofa. But I want to figure out what made her come here today. It has to be more than curiosity. "Are you in town long?"

"I live here."

I control my expression. Rory's back in L.A. and I didn't even know. I used to know everything about her, including the exact spot that made her scream. I swear it's the memories talking when I hear my own treacherous voice say, "Meet me this weekend."

Rory's about to answer when a sharp-eared kid yells, "What about Mrs. Claus? The elf is a snitch!"

This cracks Rory's facade. She laughs so hard that she snorts, and I know how rare that is. Even old Rory liked to appear in control of herself.

Except during orgasm.

More images flash through my mind. Santa should not be having those thoughts right now. "She wants to see my North Pole," I call out, enjoying the second snort I get out of Rory.

The kids chorus, "Show her! Show her!"

Rory is losing it. She keeps trying to straighten her expression, but she can't hold it. "You're terrible," she squeaks out.

"Santa has an endless amount of euphemisms." I tug a candy cane out of my ample side pocket. "Need something to suck on?" I say close to her ear.

She's dying.

"So how about it?" I ask.

I can see her debating. She presses the back of her hand to her nose to get some control, then asks, "Mrs.

Claus won't mind?" She glances down at my hand, but I'm wearing gloves. I've already checked her ring finger. Empty.

I whisper, "There is no Mrs. Claus."

I can tell from the way she shivers that this was at least part of the information she was seeking.

"All right," she says. "Is your number the same?"

"It is. I'm still in your contacts?" She never drunk-dialed me at midnight. Not in any of the ten years since our split. Of course, I never contacted her either. She was clear about making a clean break.

"You are," she says. "Let me know when you're free of this." She glances at the line. "I expect you'll be busy until Christmas."

"I'm the B Santa," I say, stroking my fake beard. "Until I grow this out."

"Are you? Growing it out?" Her gaze flitters to my jaw, and I wonder if her tastes have changed from the clean-shaven cheeks she used to run the back of her hand across. Hell yeah, I'll grow a beard for her, especially if she lets me tickle the inside of her thighs with it.

"I might."

"Message me." She walks away, and I have to force myself not to watch her glorious ass as she sashays past the food court. Santa shouldn't be looking at her like that. Not with an audience.

I turn to the line, walking forward to high-five all the kids as I make my way back to the photo set.

I'm sure between now and the time I see Rory again, I can come up with a suitable reason why I put on the red suit, one that completely avoids the sad, vulnerable truth.

Because I'm certainly not putting my heart in her hands again.

Other parts of my anatomy, though? Totally fair game.

3

RORY

I have a date with Mack McAllister.

As I head back to the office, I practically buzz with anxiety.

It's not like I've been pining for him. I've had relationships since then. Of course I have.

But nothing like him.

We were wild. Sex on the first date. On every date. Moved in together at the end of the semester. Never let an evening end or a morning begin without tumbling together in one location or the other—bed, floor, shower, kitchen table. I have a tiny scar on my hip from when we broke my glass coffee table.

We could not get enough of each other.

It would have impacted our grades, except we discovered we were ranked first and second for our year. Then the race was on to see who would come out on top. We placed bets on every exam, every mock trial. Whoever won got to dictate the next location, position, the risk level of our crazy acts.

The flashing montage in my head makes me hot all over. Whoa.

My face is flushed by the time I make it back to my office.

Jerome, my executive assistant, takes one look at me and follows me into the office with an iced frappuccino from his mini-fridge.

"If I didn't know you better, I'd think you did something dirty on your break," he says, setting the bottle on my desk.

"Hardly. Just ran into an old friend." I drop my bag on the floor. I remember the phone and tug it out. The corner of the case is crunched, but the phone itself is fine.

"An old friend, huh?" Jerome comes around the table. "What is that in your hair?" He pulls out a bit of straw. "Did you have a roll in the literal hay?"

I clap my hands to my head. "It was a hat."

"Mmm hmm. Whatever you say, boss." He backs away. "Might want to take a look before your meeting."

He's right. I head to my private bathroom and flip on the lights. My hair is a fright. I pull a brush from the cabinet to smooth it.

Jerome waits near the door. "You have calls from Wilson with the Bent Corporation about the meeting on Tuesday, and from Carl Baker's assistant making sure you get the briefs on the Penfield deal to her before EOB tomorrow."

"Is Alaina done with the briefs?" I shake my head, making sure there's nothing else in my hair. Stupid hat. I picked it up at an accessory store on the way to the Santa set. I should have known it would shed on me.

"She was working on them when I checked earlier. I'll check on it."

"Thanks." I think I have it all. I return to the office. "All good?" I ask Jerome.

He peers into my hair. He's a foot taller than me, all lean muscle and deep black skin. Dresses like a million bucks. Today he's in a blue suit with skinny pants and a salmon shirt. He could side-gig as a model if he wanted.

I stare down at his polished brown shoes while he looks. He's showing his mankles. "You're clear," he says. "I still want the deets on this little jaunt you made. I know when a woman has had her senses engaged." He shrugs. "Or a man."

Jerome is pan and poly and knows more about everything than I ever will. There's no fooling him, and a big chunk of why we work so well together is that he can figure out my mood at a glance and adjust my schedule accordingly.

So I confess. "I ran into Mack McAllister."

"The sports agent?" Jerome perches on the corner of my desk, eyes alight. "Please tell me you can get me into a party with some of his athletes. Gymnasts. Footballers. I don't discriminate."

"The one and only. And I don't run in his circles." I sit in my chair and examine the phone case again. "Can you order me a new one?" I pass it to him.

"Same color and style?"

"Yes."

He pops the case off. "You're avoiding the most important detail."

"I told you where I went."

"But not why you were as aroused as a peacock in mating season." He's not going to let this go.

"We have a history."

"You and Mack? Why do I not know this?"

I roll my chair to face my computer screen. "Because it's history."

"Not by the shade of your blush, it's not."

I shake my mouse to wake the computer. "I agreed to see him again. I'm not sure it's the best idea, though."

Jerome walks around the desk to stand behind the monitor. He's after the whole story. "Now we're getting somewhere. How long ago was this history? I've known you for four years."

"Law school. Berkeley. We were together for about two years."

"And it just ended? Poof?"

"We graduated. Went our separate ways." I glance at him for only a moment, then focus my eyes on the screen. I don't want him to think this is some big emotional blowout. "It happens all the time. I got a job in Boston. He stayed west."

"So there's about to be some rekindling going on, I take it. He never married either?"

I shrug. "He has zero personal information on the web. But he's not married currently."

"You asked?"

"He offered."

Jerome taps the top of the monitor with his finger.

"We can order prior marriage documents. It's public record."

"I'm sure I'll find it out for myself soon enough."

My phone buzzes. Jerome is still holding it. "Looks like Saturday night," he says.

I guess it's a good thing I told him, since he saw the text first. He hands the phone to me. The notification screen shows the preview of a message from Mack. *Saturday? 8?*

I tap out, *Where?*

"Like it matters with what you two are going to do," Jerome says. He's leaning over the monitor to spy.

"Hush."

The next text arrives with a buzz. *Santa Monica Pier. Ferris wheel.*

"That's romantic," Jerome says.

Is it? I find it odd, but I text, *Sure.*

"Don't sound eager or anything," Jerome says, rolling his eyes. "*Sure.* Not *yes!* Or *can't wait!* But *sure.*"

I set the phone by my keyboard. "Thanks for ordering the case. I need to review the documents for my next meeting."

"Okay, boss." He heads out again. "I better get a full rundown on Monday. And if you end up at a party with pretty people, I expect a text."

I wait for the door to close before I sag in my chair. It's hitting me, everything that's happened today.

What have I done? Agreed to a date with Mack? How is that going to end?

A rush of heat to a certain part of my body is my first clue.

4

MACK

I HAVE TO ADMIT, I HAVE TROUBLE FOCUSING AFTER Rory leaves. I can't believe she sought me out. Showed up at Riverside Mall.

Talk about the ghost of Christmas past.

But I text her during my break, and it looks like we're getting together. So I manage to get back into my Santa mindset.

Just in time, too.

A mom leads an angry, foot-dragging six-year-old boy toward me. I might have a runner. Some of them can be real fighters, too. I got punched in the gut on my first day by an eight-year-old who wanted, I kid you not, a flamethrower.

This one has his eye on the side gate. I reach into my pocket for a candy cane. Some kids get the reward at the end. Others need the bribe up front.

I hold it out. "Ho, ho, ho," I say. "Would you like a candy cane from Santa?"

He stares me down. "I don't take candy from strangers."

His mom clutches his shoulder. She's harried from standing in line, her hair mussed, her shirt askew, no doubt from tussling with this kid while they waited. She must really want her picture.

"Mitchell, he's not a stranger," she says. "He's Santa Claus!"

"I don't know him," Mitchell says.

"He comes into our house every Christmas to leave presents."

"So he's practically a criminal!"

The beard hides my smile. I love the quick thinkers. "I'm only there to fill your stocking," I tell him.

"Stockings are dumb," he says. "An Xbox doesn't even fit."

Good, good. As soon as they tell me what they're after, I can work with the situation.

I make eye contact with the mom, then ask Mitchell, "So you're hoping for an Xbox?"

She gives a quick nod, and I know this gift is part of the plan. It's infinitely harder when it's not. I'm not a Santa who promises presents that aren't going to happen.

"Who wouldn't want an Xbox?" Mitchell says with exasperation.

I'm ready for this. "Are you going to play Sonic? Spider-Man?"

"Minecraft!" he says. "I'm going to build a dungeon like my friend Joe!"

I relax now that the dialogue has begun. The hard

part is over. I lean close. "What did Steve say to the skeleton?"

He seems surprised I know who the main character of Minecraft is. "I don't know."

"I have a bone to pick with you."

Mitchell rolls his eyes.

I slide right into the next one. "Why didn't the skeleton fight back?"

But Mitchell knows this one. His face lights up. "Because he didn't have the guts!"

"That's right!"

The kid cracks a smile.

Time to get Mom's picture. "Can I tell you my Minecraft secret?"

Mitchell steps forward, and he's in camera range. Bingo. I cup my white-gloved hand near his ear. This is a favorite pose, Santa talking to a kid. Mom will love it. "I once built six mega-fortresses just so I could blow them up with TNT."

His eyes get big. "How long did that take?"

"Two days."

He glances around to see if his mother is listening. She's filming with her phone.

I've got him now. It's my job to keep the magic going. Convince the unbelievers. Soothe the ones with troubles they bring to me. I've only been at this gig two weeks, and already I've been asked for moms to get out of the hospital, for dads to return home. To bring back beloved pets that died.

It can be hard.

I never thought I'd be good at it. Kids weren't my

thing. Comes with the territory of being the second of ten. My whole childhood was spent raising siblings. By the time I left home for college, I was over it.

But here I am.

Mitchell leans in close, and I know I'm about to get an earful about why he was so upset walking up. "Mom says I can't have an Xbox unless I'm good."

Ahh. Lots of kids walk up with this chip on their shoulder. "You think that's a problem? You don't think you're good?"

His soulful eyes meet mine. "Maybe not always."

I nod. "I understand. But there's something your mom has forgotten."

He grips my hand, and we're on the verge of the breakthrough, helping him sort the competing Christmas messages. Rich and poor. Deserving and undeserving. Money spent equals love. He's old enough to have started seeing the hypocrisy.

"What did she forget?" he asks.

I give him a wink and point at my chest. "I'm the one who decides who's naughty or nice."

I hold out my fist for a bump, and he knocks his against mine. I think we're done, and the mother is practically sparkling with happiness at the images when he throws himself against me for a hug.

Funny how it works. It's a rare kid who doesn't believe in the magic when they look it in the face. They want to believe. They want to feel the joy.

It's a demanding job helping them get there.

It's the best job.

The mom walks up to lead Mitchell off the set so

she can buy her images. I glance out at the line. It's not quite wrapped around the train anymore. There will be a slight slowdown during the height of traffic, a small break before the evening Santa arrives. He's the experienced one with a real beard.

I'm tired. The bulky suit with its cooling vest and fake belly is wearing on me. But another kid is coming, and each one has waited a long time to see me. I need to give them my full attention.

But even so, ever lurking in the back of my mind is Rory.

Two more days, and I get to see her.

5

RORY

22 Days to Christmas

My gold bracelets jingle as I maneuver my car into the parking lot below the Santa Monica Pier. The beach and boardwalk are busy on a Saturday night, and I have to hunt for a spot.

It's Southern California, so most of the people walking around wear some variation of bathing suit and cover-up, even in December.

I chose a striped cotton skirt a touch shorter than I would wear to work, and a lush silvery-gray sweater that falls off one shoulder. That's about as casual as I get.

My dark hair is twisted into a comb. If I dared to leave it down this close to the ocean, it would kink into an unruly mass no matter how many products I slathered into it. Even with my efforts, curls are tightening into coils around my forehead.

I check the rearview mirror before I leave the car.

My makeup is on point. I wish I didn't have a resting Grinch face. *Smile, Rory. Don't look like you're about to destroy him in court.*

I take my time walking up the steps to the pier. Meet at the Ferris wheel, Mack said. What a bizarre, romantic notion. It seems further proof he's going through some sentimental midlife crisis.

The crowd grows thick as I start down the wood planks of the boardwalk. It's gaudy and loud, all kitschy souvenir stands and food to eat standing up.

But I can't deny the happy energy. My childhood didn't involve many days at beaches or amusement parks. Mom wasn't into unbridled leisure. She was a workaholic who raised me to be one, too.

Despite my upbringing, I understand the appeal. Dig into the sand. Eat a cone full of spun sugar. Scramble your insides with a death-defying ride. It can take your mind off your troubles, if only for a day.

Except I'm the sort who faces my troubles head-on. Mack McAllister is currently one of them.

I tug my phone from my purse, ready to text Mack. He's absolutely mad to think we'll be able to find each other in this crowd.

I didn't get a clear look at him due to the Santa suit. What if he's really aged? What if I'm wrong about the ripped abs?

My steps falter. I don't care if Mack is different. Of course not. Besides, this is a fact-finding mission. It's not a hookup.

I spot him. He's leaning against the blue pillar holding the sign to Pacific Park. The vividly painted shops, umbrella-covered tables, lights, noise, and people fade out as if they don't exist.

Mack is almost completely unchanged by the intervening years. His eyebrows stand out, dark and expressive. And although I can't see the color of his eyes from this distance, I know exactly their shade of green.

The pale blue polo shirt is tailored to fit his broad shoulders. And he was definitely wearing a belly pillow when I saw him as Santa. Everything about him is muscled and fit. I shiver remembering all the ways I manhandled that body. It was once mine to do with as I pleased.

My feet have sped up of their own accord, eager to reach him. He's seen me, and I'm drawn to his gaze like a tractor beam.

If I follow my urge right now, I'll tackle him. I stop several feet away to avoid the intense pull of his magnetism. I had no idea he'd make me feel this way once we were away from the kids and his Santa gear.

"Rory," he says, and my name on his lips knocks me completely off-center, not that I was balanced before.

When I first try to respond, my throat is knotted up. I forgot what this feeling is like. Being near Mack is a full-body experience.

"Hello," I finally manage. "Quite a spot."

He glances around, as if only now considering his choice. "I like it. It's a great mix of people. Young. Old. In between." He looks to me then, and I understand what he's saying. We were young once, and not quite old now. But different from before.

He turns to face the bright noise of the amusement park. "Shall we shake things up?"

"Maybe." I follow him into the chaotic section of the pier, the roller coaster rumbling over our heads.

He pauses at the ticket booth at the base of the Ferris wheel.

"Fancy a ride into the sky?" he asks. "Perfect view of the ocean."

I follow his gaze to the towering circle of umbrella-covered cars. It spins into the darkening sky with a dazzle of lights.

The line is moderately long, and I see that this is an opportunity for a lengthy talk. Mack always was clever. He thought this one through.

"Sure," I tell him. Although *sure* is something I'm not. I have a healthy fear of heights. I think being in the car will be fine. It's not like I'll be standing on a ledge.

But here I go. Doing two scary things at once. An amusement park ride and a conversation with Mack McAllister after a decade of silence.

Once we have tickets, we take our place in line. People stretch along a queue surrounded by rides moving and blinking in every direction. I have to resist the urge to duck every time the roller coaster crosses over our heads.

I'm unsure of what to say next. I'm wildly curious about the Santa gig, but I can't quite find the words to ask my question.

Mack seems content to look around, occasionally pausing on my face. Maybe he's just as unsure. The silence is out of character for us both, but then, we did blow up spectacularly ten years ago.

I opt to go with a safe topic, friends from our past. "Do you hear much from Marta or Henry or Jenessa?"

He smiles, and I'm struck by how familiar his expression is. "Sure. Henry and I meet to watch a ball game about once a month. I haven't talked directly to Marta or Jen in a while, but I saw online that Jen had a baby a couple of months ago."

"Did she?" I try to picture the crazy woman who always did shots in dive bars holding a baby instead.

Mack tilts his head quizzically. "You don't keep up with anyone?"

My chest tightens. I don't. And I can see that looks bad to him.

I rush to explain. "None of them went into corporate law." Instantly, I regret saying it. It sounds like they aren't important enough to talk to because they aren't part of my career.

Is it true?

I don't have time to think about it, because Mack says, "You always were the networker."

Before I can ask what he means, or even glean whether it's an insult or a compliment, he goes on. "I regret losing touch with Saul." His face is solemn.

I agree with that. "He left for the Peace Corps and that was it."

"Goes to show, the legal rat race isn't for everyone."

We take several steps forward. The wind picks up, pulling more errant curls from my hair. "Such a shame. Saul was brilliant."

Mack frowns. "I'm sure he's being brilliant wherever he is."

Dang. I can't say anything right. Maybe I shouldn't have come. So what if Mack is a Santa now? What business is it of mine? I should have left us in the past. All I can do at this point is confirm we were never the right fit.

But we're stuck between metal fences lined with mesh, a long line ahead and behind. My last attempt at jumping a divider to escape Mack didn't end well.

In front of us, a teen girl leans her head on a boy's shoulder, their hands clasped between them. A wave of melancholy washes across me. Did Mack and I look like that to outsiders? I don't think so. They're so connected, so close.

Mack and I always had a hefty mutual respect. And definitely an addiction to each other's bodies. But we were never what you would call *sweet on each other*.

Mack turns and catches me watching. "Young love," he says quietly.

I avoid his gaze, instead staring up at the giant wheel. I'm not ready to be hit with what I've never had. The night sky deepens to black behind the vivid display of lights and patterns.

"Have you done it before?" Mack asks. I hesitate, thinking he is talking about love, but he adds, "The Pacific Wheel, I mean."

My shoulders relax with relief. "No. The only time I came to the pier was for a business retreat. We didn't ride any of the attractions."

Mack points up at the giant wheel. "Did you know that this is Iron Man's favorite ride?"

I'm confused. "Do you mean the comic book character or Robert Downey Jr.?"

He grins. "Either one. It's a *ferrous* wheel."

I drop my jaw. *Ferris. Ferrous.* Ferrous is iron. "Did you just tell me a dad joke?"

"Well, I *am* Father Christmas."

"Oh my God." I groan, but Mack has given me the opening I've been looking for. "So why are you doing it? Are your clients starting to look for someone more family-friendly? Do they need a kid-first publicity angle from you?"

He rocks back on his heels. "Rory Sheffield. Always looking for an angle."

"What's wrong with that? I'm trying to understand how it benefits you to take a side job so far out of your career path."

His gaze pierces me, sharp and true as an arrow. "Why would you even care? It's not like you ever looked back after you left."

Ouch. "If you're so mad after all this time, why am I here?" Heat rises in my cheeks.

"I believe you were the one who found me."

"I believe you were the one who asked to see me tonight," I shoot back.

The couple in front of us glances behind. I clench my jaw. I hate being a public spectacle.

Mack shoves his hands in his pockets, back to watching the lighted wheel. His mannerisms have changed. He was always so self-possessed. The Mack I knew didn't fidget.

"What happened to you?" I realize too late how harsh the question sounds. I bring it down. "What I mean is, you were always such a tiger."

"And now I'm a pussycat?" His green eyes lock on mine.

"Is the Mack I used to know buried in crushed velvet and fur?"

A gap has formed in front of us, and Mack moves us forward to close it. "Let me ask you a question." His voice has an edge, like he might use in a courtroom. He's redirecting me.

I almost want to say, "I object," but suspect it will sound more like Reese Witherspoon in *Legally Blonde* than the put-together image I'm going for. So I wait.

His face is earnest when he asks, "Do you think you're more of what you were when you started out as a lawyer, or less?"

"What do you mean by 'more of what you were'? I know more. Have more experience. So I guess I'm more."

He shakes his head. "No, I mean more of what makes you, well, *you*. Are you more ambitious? More aggressive? Or have you evened out? Has the world shown you other ways to be?"

That's a loaded question. "I try to stay focused," I say. "I've done a better job at balancing work and leisure."

His eyebrow quirks. "In what way?"

"I have a dog."

Now he's grinning. "You? A dog?"

We move forward, entering the loading zone. A man gestures us to a yellow chain.

"His name is Sir Winston. He's a black lab and the love of my life."

I realize I have perhaps shared too much, and snap my mouth closed.

Mack's grin is even wider. "The love of your life?"

The wheel turns, and the red umbrella car that's meant for us slides into place. The man holds his hand up for us to wait as the couple who was in the car before exits the other side.

When it's empty, Mack leads the way into the car. He sits on one of the plastic seats, and I choose to sit opposite him. Balance the load.

He seems amused by this. As the tiny doors swing closed, Mack leans forward, his elbows on his knees. "I've changed. I haven't gone as far as a dog, like you. Amazing, by the way, given your dislike of dogs when we were together."

"I didn't dislike them," I counter. "I wasn't in a place to have one in my apartment. They were expensive. And messy. And you couldn't leave them and jet away for a weekend."

He sits back, watching me. "But we never did that, did we? Just go away for a weekend?"

"We were students. Busy and poor."

The wheel moves, the wind whipping his hair as we rise above the buildings.

It's instantly colder, and I'm glad for the sweater as I wrap my arms around my waist. But I was right about the height. As long as the umbrella provides a smooth and even ride, it's fine that we're in the air. I avoid taking in too much of the horizon.

"So what has changed about you exactly?" I ask. We're about to get to the meat of what I want to know. What turned Mack into Santa.

He runs his hands through his hair, staring out at the dark, endless sea.

I wait. This is important. Maybe with my questions answered, I can put my thoughts of Mack to rest. I dislike the pang of regret that sometimes pierces me when he crosses my mind. Perhaps after tonight, I can let all that go.

"I want more," Mack says. "So much more."

Back to that. "More of what?"

He refuses to look at me, his gaze on the ocean. "Everything. I want more of everything."

"And Santa gives you that?"

"It does."

I let out a long sigh. Mack is talking in riddles, and I'm stuck on a Ferris wheel with him.

6

MACK

RORY SHEFFIELD IS DOING WHAT SHE ALWAYS DOES, going for the jugular. She thinks my Santa work is some logical career pivot. She can't believe anything that doesn't match her worldview.

I should've expected that. I sit back on the hard plastic seat, trying to look casual and relaxed. She watches me from her side of the car, her hands clasped tightly together, her elbows drawn against her body. You could bounce a quarter off the tension in her shoulders. You always could.

I decide if she can quiz me about my Santa gig, I'm going to ask her what I want to know.

"So anyone important in your life other than Sir Winston?" I doubt it, since she's out with me. But she could have agreed to this excursion with the ridiculous notion that we could be friends.

She tightens up even more compactly into her gray sweater ball. This question unnerves her and she's all out of redirects. Interesting.

Her position across from me provides an incredible view of her long legs. I remember running my tongue along every inch of them. The visions are seared into my brain. I can't stop overlaying our history on top of the woman she is now. There has been no woman like her, ever.

"I've been in several relationships," she says finally, her eyes daring me to question it. As if I'd know. "No one currently."

"How long since the last?" It's not even a fair question, but I feel like going there. The idea that she's been with someone else, anyone, sends a fire raging through me. That's why I never looked at her social media. I didn't want to see.

"Why should it matter to you?" Her eyes spark fire, and I should heed the warning, but instead, I plunge forward.

"I'm wondering how sloppy the seconds are."

"Oh my God. What the hell, Mack!" She leans to one side of the car as if she can escape me.

I should backtrack. Apologize. But I don't. I foolishly dash ahead like a crazy man aiming for a cliff. "Were any of them half as good as we were together?"

"You have no right to ask any of this!" She slides to the end of the bench to put more distance between us.

We glide to a stop to load more riders, and the car tilts with the shift of her weight. It's not much, but she bumps against the wall of the car, making it rock.

This triggers something in her eyes, and she clutches her side of the car. This movement makes the umbrella rock again. "Why are we stopped?" She sucks in a breath. "Are we stuck?" She presses her hand to her chest. She can't seem to exhale.

"Rory?"

I shift toward her, but this sends the car even more off balance. Rory yelps.

The tilt isn't that dramatic. There's no way to make the car swing in a dangerous way. But it's enough to scare her.

I shift to the opposite end of my seat to balance out the weight.

Even as the car levels out, her breath wheezes in and out.

"Rory?"

She doesn't respond. The terror in her eyes cuts me to the core.

"Are you afraid of heights?" I can't move even the smallest bit without creating a shift in the car. Around us, other riders shout and rock their cars for a thrill.

She doesn't glance my way, her gaze fixed on the shore, the dull white lights stretching out, a stark comparison to the bright, flickering neon all around us. She gasps to draw in air.

"Rory!" I say louder, hoping to startle her into breathing right, into listening to me.

We have twenty minutes on this thing, easy. It's why I chose it. In case we got into a battle. It would force us to work it out. They have to load the rest of the cars, then run the full circle, which will dramatically pick up its pace. If she can't handle sitting here, I'm not sure what she'll do during the speedy parts.

I didn't anticipate this.

The car starts to move again, the next riders on board. It will only go about halfway around before its next stop.

Rory whimpers, hand to her chest, her eyes closed. My heart turns over. I had no idea this would terrify her.

With the wheel turning, our movements in the car are less noticeable. I brace my feet on the floor, and in one swift shift of weight, I switch to the other side.

The seat rocks slightly, and Rory's eyes fly open. But I grasp her arm and pull her to me, situating us in the center of the seat, tightly squeezed together.

"You're all right," I say. "Breathe with me, okay?" Her face is a tight mask of fear. I press her head into my shoulder. "Listen to my heartbeat," I tell her. "Feel me breathe."

I went to Santa School to ensure I'd be able to land a job. I had no other work experience with kids. Part of the training was helping hysterical children calm down, as well as keeping yourself chill during difficult moments.

Breath is the key element. Telling your body to breathe reminds your brain that you are in control. That you're okay. I used the strategies I learned on the very first day of my Santa job and for every shift since.

"In," I say. "Hold it at the top. And out."

I can feel her chest moving. Something is happening.

Holding her has its effect on me. I forgot what it was like to have Rory in my arms. She tucks her head beneath my chin in a way I'd long forgotten. Loose curls tickle my jaw.

Her body starts to relax.

The wheel makes several starts and stops as she slowly calms. Finally, it picks up speed, going through its spinning stage. The cold wind whips at us, and I pull her tight.

"We shouldn't fight," she says, and I'm relieved she can speak again. Her breath is back.

"We shouldn't. I'm sorry I said all that."

"All that time we were rivals, and we never had a fight." She buries her face into my chest.

"Because it was us against the world, even when we were trying to outscore each other on exams."

"We're on our own now," she says. "It's no longer you and me."

The world whirls by as we spin and spin. She doesn't look, her face in my chest, her arms around me. I hold on to her, and it feels as if each pass around the wheel is another year of our lives. They flew by, barely noticed. I didn't know to look, to see the sights, to hold on.

But now she's here. I shouldn't care where she's been in our time apart. That's petty, and it's not like I was a saint.

"I guess I shouldn't tell you why a Ferris wheel is like an elevator."

She huffs a laugh. "Is it a good joke, at least?"

"I think so. They both work on so many levels."

She shakes her head against my chest, mussing her perfect hair. She's more like my Rory now, and I will relish this moment to hold her like I once could.

Maybe someday soon, I can tell her why I'm Santa. Right now I'm not prepared to lay my heart bare to her, not when she's the same career-focused woman who chose life without me.

But it's Christmas, and it feels like anything can happen. Maybe unlike the years that spun into oblivion, I can make this season last. And if I have enough time, maybe Rory and I can find some new way to be a team. We're in the same part of the world again. There's nothing stopping us.

She tells me I've changed, and of course I have. I first put on the red suit two months ago and sat in a room alongside two hundred other Santas.

My classmates teased me for my youth, my lack of beard, my dark hair. But my instructors told me I would have decades in the chair if I wanted it, and the only real qualification for the job was a commitment to spreading the joy of Christmas. The hair and the beard can be bought, even good enough to survive the hard tug of a child.

And I had what mattered—the heart of St. Nick.

It's no surprise to me that being Santa has brought Rory back to me.

Once you believe in the magic, anything can happen.

7
RORY

When we finally get off the Ferris wheel, two things have happened. One, I can breathe again. I had no idea I was going to fully panic on that ride.

Two, Mack and I are holding hands. The connection we felt on the ride can't be ignored. And I see no need to hold myself apart from him. We're Mackory again, the power couple, top of our class. If tonight is nothing more than an homage to that, it's okay.

"I say we get off the pier," Mack says. "Go someplace quiet."

"Okay."

He's feeling guilty that he dragged me on the ride. And maybe that he didn't know such an important thing about me.

But I always hid my weaknesses. My mother taught me that. And there was no other occasion for Mack to know I got panicky with heights. To be honest, I didn't know it could get that bad myself.

We drive together in Mack's sleek black Maserati.

This is the car of a sports agent, for sure, designed to reel in impressionable young athletes to the fame and fortune in their future if they sign.

It's also sexy as hell. I glance in the back seat, torturing myself with visions of Mack and some other woman trysting there. But there isn't one. I sigh in relief. I get an inkling of why he reacted so strongly to me saying there were other men. I feel it, too. Like he should have been mine.

I have no idea if Mack is as wild with everyone as he was with me. We did a lot more than back seats. Nowhere was off-limits, especially if one of us lost a bet or got a lower grade. The winner chose the time, the place, and the body parts involved.

The memories flush me with heat again. I've never been able to re-create that feeling with anyone else. Not even close.

I force myself to think of other things. Not sexy cars. Not sexy Mack. Not sex with Mack. Outside the windows, the lights of Santa Monica are bright. "I rarely come down here," I say. "It's pretty."

"I like it."

"Do you live close?"

His gaze remains on the road as he makes a turn. "Yeah. I have a condo a few miles from here."

"I live in L.A. proper."

"When did you leave Boston?"

"Four years ago."

He goes silent, and I know he's thinking that I could have contacted him. And I thought about it when I returned. But it had been six years by then. There hadn't seemed to be a point.

"Your drawl is less than it was," I say, just to fill the empty air.

Mack pulls into a parking lot of a place called the Seafood Shack. "Happens when you don't go home a lot."

He slides into a spot and opens his door. It's wild, this car, with the doors that fly up rather than push out. By the time my foot hits the pavement, he's there, extending a hand, helping me up.

I don't need to ask him why he doesn't go home much. I never met his family, not in the two years we were together. He was bitter about his youth spent caring for a passel of kids. He didn't get to do extracurriculars or play sports. I'm not sure he even made prom.

We enter the shack, noise blasting as soon as Mack opens the door. The hostess waves like she knows him and leads us to a table.

"What is this place?" I ask. The well-dressed, highly polished clientele doesn't match the rough plank floor, sagging fishnets on the walls, and dilapidated booths.

"It's one of those places that's basically nothing great, but it's impossible to get a table because celebrities crash it for its local feel."

The hostess gestures at a booth. "For you, Mr. McAllister."

"Thanks," he says.

He must come here often. I slide onto the bench. The food options are printed on ragged plastic-covered menus.

I glance around. It's full of power couples, model types, actors, and older men who seem very sure of themselves. I know the type. I defend them in court cases.

There isn't a kid in the place. This seems like an old Mack restaurant, not the Santa version. But I'm not going to quiz him on this. We've said enough on that subject for one night.

We order drinks and food. "You're quieter than you were in law school," Mack says.

He's pegged me. I straighten my knife and fork next to my plate. "I try to think before I speak now."

"That's new." He looks amused as he takes a bite of bread.

"I'm different in a lot of ways." It's time to be a grownup. I draw in a breath for courage. "Mack, I want to apologize for how I left things. I was so focused that I left you after graduation without a proper ending."

He sets the chunk of bread down, eyes on his plate. "I'd like to say it didn't matter, but it did. I thought I'd done something terrible to make you not even want me to follow you to Boston." His green gaze meets mine. "I would have followed you."

"I know." I twist the linen napkin in my lap. "I felt the job offer you had here in California was the logical one. I didn't want to get in your way. We had a long way to go to know where we'd land in our careers."

He holds my gaze. "I accept your apology."

A heaviness lifts from my chest. I should have done that a long time ago. Instead I left him and all our former friends behind. There was no one to tell me how he'd fared. Or to draw me back. I threw myself into my work.

I snag a bit of bread myself, suddenly hungry. "So tell me everything that's happened since we graduated. Leave nothing out."

The waiter brings our drinks, and I sip mine, watching him over the rim.

Mack rolls his beer bottle between his palms. "I took the agency internship. Mostly did background work, then one of the lead agent's clients refused to re-sign with him."

Ooh. Work dirt. I lean forward. "Was it over money?"

"I think he'd made some unwanted gestures."

"Gross."

"Right? It's such a problem in sports."

"A problem everywhere."

He nods. "Because I had done the original paperwork, I knew this athlete had a big event coming up. If she did well, tons of endorsement offers would come in."

"All new contracts, which a second agent could negotiate."

"Exactly. I made her an offer, and she took it. But I had to quit my old job. I wasn't allowed to take anyone with me, so I branched out on my own with my future pinned on a nineteen-year-old tennis player."

I had no idea this happened. Agents aren't part of my legal circles. "Don't keep me in suspense."

"She nailed it. We got six deals. It was enough to keep me afloat while I signed some other tennis stars.

Then one of them started dating a football player, and he was about to get drafted. So I got my first pro football contract. And suddenly I had big deals on my desk as he mentioned me to his teammates."

"How do you have time to be Santa?"

"I hired some staff. Took on a junior agent. There's only a couple of clients who need handholding this season."

Our food arrives. The cracked crab is buttery, and the roasted garlic mashed potatoes smell heavenly. I take a bite and almost swoon. "It's so good."

"I'd make a crab joke here, but——"

I hold up a hand. "Please don't."

"I'm not sure I can stop it."

I shake my head. Mack was always glib, but the joke-telling is new. "All right. But only one."

He stares at the table a moment. "I have so many, I can't pick just one."

"Only one."

"All right. Why didn't the crab share his French fries?"

"Oh, God."

"Because he was shellfish!"

"Mack."

"What does a crab call his house?"

"Mack! Only one!"

"Mi-chelle!"

"No more!"

"Just one more."

"Mack."

His gorgeous, chiseled face is alight with happiness. I've never seen him like this.

"Okay," I say. "Go on."

"Crabs hate lifting weights. They always pull a mussel."

What have I done?

He keeps going. "Crabs are great at social media. They take the best shelfies on their shell phones."

"No puns."

He glares at me.

"A girl has standards!"

He laughs. "I've worked up an appetite."

"Finally." But inside, I feel happy. The tension seems to have melted away. Like my butter. Oh no, I'm starting to think in dad jokes! I quickly stuff my face with a forkful of potatoes.

We settle into the food for a moment, then he asks, "So what about you? How did you fare after graduation?"

I take a sip of my drink. "Very typical trajectory. Drudge work for years. Worked up until I had a better title. Then took that title and moved to a medium-sized firm willing to make me a partner."

"So you're already a partner?"

I sit a little taller. "I am."

"Wow."

"Well, you own the whole agency on your end."

Mack sits back in his chair. "I guess you were right. Separating made us successful." But despite his praise, his tone isn't quite right.

He's back to thinking of my departure. I twist the napkin beneath the table. "I like to believe so."

"Now what?" His question hangs over the table like the aftermath of a clap of thunder. The storm is here.

"Does there have to be a plan?"

"I suppose not."

We've gone up and down the range of emotions tonight. I suppose it could only be that way, given so much history, and all the silence in between.

The waiter takes our dishes, and we're quiet while Mack settles the check. I wonder if this is all there's going to be, this one night to close out the time we were together.

We don't hold hands on the way back to the car, and the drive back to the beach is silent. Mack turns on the radio, and obviously the universe knows we've found each other, because immediately Lady Gaga's "You and I" starts to play.

As soon as the lyrics roll, Mack catches my eye. There's something so different about him. He takes things in. They affect him.

The song gets to me. It applies to us so much more than it did ten years ago. This thing we used to be, all sex and competition and focus, is returning in some strange new combination.

There's emotion now. I give a damn about what he's feeling.

And in a minute, we're going to get to the part of the song where I know *exactly* what he's thinking about.

8

MACK

THIS SONG. DAMN.

It was all over the radio back then. I try to focus on the road, but visions are filling my head.

I haven't heard this song much in the intervening years. But when I do, I always think of Rory.

It was playing on our first date. We'd known each other a while in class. The rivalry was thick already. We'd been doing research on a legal brief for days, holed up in the library with Saul and Jenessa.

Jenessa said, "You two are the most intense people in our year."

Saul agreed.

I never thought of myself as intense. I got through undergrad on scholarship by the seat of my pants, trying to fill in holes in my education as I went along. Law school had only been a pipe dream, but after a couple of years working and applying, I'd made it.

I had to work for every small thing. I certainly didn't

have a legacy of educated people in my family to lead the way.

But if what Jenessa said was true, that this beautiful woman sitting across the desk from me was as intense as I was, then we should lean into it.

I looked at her and said, "I think we should get out of here."

Jenessa elbowed Saul with a nod. Clearly everyone expected this.

Rory watched me for a moment, as if trying to make a decision. I didn't know much about her outside of class. Hell, she could've had a boyfriend and I wouldn't have had a clue.

But she slowly nodded and, with careful deliberation, began packing her books into her backpack.

I was outrageously broke, trying to minimize my student loan debt as I paid my way through school. So our first day alone together wasn't much more than walking through campus and picking up sandwiches at one of the cafés.

But the conversation was fierce. It started with our classwork and veered into philosophy.

From there we went into religion's impact on morality and the law, then skated straight into the *Kama Sutra* somehow. Once our conversation went in that direction, there was no stopping my wild imagination about what to do to Rory.

I almost miss my turn in the Maserati and have to whip the car into the left lane.

"You're deep in thought," Rory says. "What's on your mind?"

Might as well confess. "Our first date." I look to the radio. "The song, you know."

"I know," she says quietly.

"I remember the backside of the stadium. The wood benches."

The light flashes on her face as we drive, and I catch a grin. "Those saw a fair bit of action from us."

"Remember when Professor Horowitz almost caught us?"

She laughs. "My prompt expulsion from law school flashed before my eyes."

Now I laugh. "Maybe. He was a perv. He might've watched."

She shakes her head. "If you say so."

"I know so. He hit on a lot of girls in our class."

Her jaw drops. "You never told me that. He never hit on me!"

"Because I would've killed him with my bare hands."

She huffs. "He didn't even know we were together."

"Everyone knew we were together, Rory."

She fiddles with her skirt. "Probably so."

"You weren't sure about me at first." I can picture how she drew in a shuddering breath as I moved toward her on that bench. Almost as if she was afraid of what we were about to become.

"I was pretty inexperienced, if you will remember." She turns to me in the dark.

"I remember." I spot the road that will lead back to the beach. The picture of Rory just before our first kiss hovers in my mind. Her hair was longer than it is now, curling onto her shoulders and down her back.

Her honey-brown eyes always paid attention, and on that bench twelve years ago, she lifted them to mine as if unsure she could put her trust in me.

Rory had a tough shell. She talked loud and never backed down. She could be prickly.

That first kiss was probably the only time I saw uncertainty in her. Dark had fallen. The night was quiet and still, few students about so late on a weeknight. The explicit conversation had done a number on me, and I wanted to hold her close.

When we sat on the wood bench, I pulled her tightly against me. And that was when I saw it, that hesitation. She was thinking, questioning, not barreling forward in a mad rush like usual.

Somebody opened a window in the International House, which was right behind us, and the Lady Gaga song was playing. Rory relaxed against my shoulder, her hand on my chest. She was in.

The moment my mouth landed on hers, all doubt evaporated. She was as hungry as I was, following my lead. If I knew in that moment she was a virgin, things might have gone differently. But when she put her arms around my neck and arched to me, I moved fast.

I slid my hands beneath her shirt, savoring the smooth feel of her skin for the first time. Her bra was dainty, and I unhooked it easily, filling my palm with her warm, full breast.

She groaned against my mouth. I wanted to touch her everywhere. The bench was secluded enough, far from the streetlight. I unbuttoned her jeans and slid my hand inside her panties.

She was so wet. I couldn't maneuver too far in this position, but I circled the nub of her clit, relishing the way her breath sped up. She gripped the back of my head, her fingers digging into my hair. I loved it.

She shuddered around me, so lightning quick, so hot. She moved her face to my shoulder, muffling the sounds she made as she orgasmed against my fingers. I pressed my hand against her, holding tight, until her quivering stilled.

"Shit, Mack," she said. "What aren't you good at?"

I threw back my head and laughed, a good, hearty release. Then I leaned in. "Wouldn't you like to know?"

"I would," she said. "Let's go somewhere that won't get me expelled."

We separated, straightening our clothes. "Public indecency," I said. "I think we know enough that we could fight the charges."

She bumped her shoulder against mine as we walked hand in hand. "Let's not push our luck."

But we would, again and again.

She wanted to go to her apartment. She had only one roommate, while I had three. We barely made it inside the door when the clothes started coming off.

I jerked her shirt over her head. Her bra was still undone. I sent it flying and feasted on her breasts as we walked together, me forward, her backward, across the living room.

We stumbled on the glass coffee table that we would later break, but that night it lived to see another sunrise.

Rory met every move of mine with her own, pulling

my shirt over my head. I kicked off my shoes in her hallway, and she left hers by her bedroom door.

I was desperate to have her in every way possible, but I might have played the next part differently if I knew she'd never done this before. The way she jerked my pants open made me feel like she wanted it fast and rough.

I grabbed her by the hips, hoisting her up and flinging her onto the bed.

I yanked her jeans to her knees and pulled them off both legs. I revisited all the spots I had just started to get to know. Her mouth, the sweet curve of her neck, down her collarbone, and landing on the taut nipple of a naked breast.

Her back arched to me, a long groan escaping her lips. I loved the feeling of her shuddering around my fingers on the bench. I wanted to feel it again, this time with my mouth.

I made my way down, dipping my tongue into the hollow of her belly button.

She clutched my head. "Yessss," she said as I nipped my way down and dragged the panties away. They hit the floor in a whisper of lace.

I shifted on the bed, knocking her thighs apart with my elbow. She gave a startled cry, but I dropped down, my mouth on her, sliding my tongue inside those wet folds.

"Oh my God, Mack!"

I was relentless, cupping her ass to lift her to me. I moved swift and hard, sucking tightly on her clit.

She bucked and shuddered. I looked up at her with her eyes closed, her hands gripping the sheets.

Her body began that quivering I already recognized. She panted, jerking the sheets off the corners of the bed. I moved faster, harder, reaching up to pinch a nipple. She screamed this time, no longer trying to avoid attention on a public bench. The pulsing began, strong and hard against my mouth. I had her.

She let out a long, deep groan and finally collapsed back down on the bed. "Mack, Mack, Mack," she said. "What are you doing to me?"

I crawled back up to her, dragging my mouth across her body as I went. "We're just getting started."

I unbuttoned my jeans and extracted my wallet before sliding them off. "Condoms okay by you?" I asked her.

She nodded, her arm across her face. She seemed spent, but I could get more from her.

I grasped her hips and flipped her over in one quick move. She let out a started cry. I pulled her hips back so her curvy ass was flush against my belly. "Is this way all right?"

"Yes," she said, and shoved back against me as if to prove it.

Looking back on this night, I often wondered if I'd fingered her first, I would have known. I hadn't dived in deep on the bench, hanging out on her clit. And tongues only reach so far.

But I had no idea, and held on to her hips as I thrust inside her in one fast push.

She did not cry out, gave no signal of distress. She

met me move for move, backing into me, taking it deeper. I grabbed her hair and pulled it back, and she groaned, loving it, urging me to move harder, faster.

I reached around her to bring our end together, but she moved my hand away and kept our rhythm, solid and unrelenting.

I unleashed and fell on her back. We both collapsed to the bed. She laughed then, a sound I've never forgotten. "Mack Squared, you're a good time," she said.

I wondered if she did this a lot. She was so into it. So willing. When we rolled over on the bed and I saw the blood on the sheets where she'd landed, I knew exactly what it meant. If she was on her period, I would have known an hour ago.

"Shit, Rory?" I looked up from the smear. She was staring down at it quizzically.

But she was logical to a fault, even then. "I wasn't sure that would happen. It doesn't always. Did you know some women don't even have a hymen? Really screwed up their lives if they were in a patriarchal or tribal society that required proof of virginity."

She went on about violence against women with purity tests, and I could barely see for the haze in my eyes.

"Rory, I was rough. I could have been gentle."

She smacked my chest. "I loved it. Couldn't have asked for a better first. Next time we can do that simultaneous thing you were going for."

I dragged her against me while she chatted on and on about the legal brief we'd been working on the library, as if everything in between had been inconsequential.

But she'd given her virginity to me. I kissed her hair and tuned back in. Eventually I understood that this was simply Rory. The facts were plain and sex was good. It remained that way for our final two years of school, until she left.

We make it back to the beach. The pier is alight, but foot traffic is less. The shore is almost deserted. It gets cold once the sun goes down.

"You still thinking about that first night?" Rory asks.

"I was."

"That was so wild. A cherry popper to go down in history."

I can't believe she takes it so lightly. "I was honored."

"It was a good run." Her voice is light, but my throat tightens.

"It was."

I want to say, *What now?* But I can't make the words come.

She watches me in the dark. I can feel her gaze even though her face is in shadow. "You're so different. I don't remember a sentimental Mack."

"Maybe you just never saw it."

"But you wouldn't go home—you skipped holidays and threw yourself into your studies."

"That was how I coped. Until I couldn't anymore, after you left."

"Are you saying I broke your heart?" Her voice tells me she doesn't believe it.

"I would have followed you."

She slaps her hands on her thighs. "But that wasn't logical! You were destined to be an agent! No telling what random job you would have taken if you'd gone to Boston!"

"Some things aren't logical," I tell her.

"I know! Like you right now!"

I can't take one more moment, so I do the only thing that feels right. I strip off my seatbelt and lean over the center console to give her the kiss of her life.

9

RORY

I forgot what kissing Mack McAllister is like.

He comes on me like a jaguar, leaning across his car with a low, sexy growl.

His lips are exactly as I remember, firm but tender.

I've had quite a few kisses in the intervening years, but none like this. Mack's kiss is the one I measured all the others against—and I found them lacking.

He slides his hand up the loose sleeve of my sweater. I feel aloft, like I'm no longer in the seat of a Maserati. There's no sensation other than Mack's mouth on mine.

I intend to hold myself apart from him. To enjoy the kiss without expanding it.

But his mouth is warm and gently explores mine. My body's memory of feeling safe in his arms is too recent, too perfect. I lean in.

The kiss is a renewal of us, tongues reunited. I reach over to squeeze his muscled, strong arm. I'm not sure anymore about holding myself aloof. Why did I want that? Our separation no longer makes sense.

The pulse of my need starts to beat low in my belly, spreading throughout my body. I remember this feeling. I will have to rein it in, or we will be repeating some of our greatest hits. Sex on the beach. Sex in cars. Sex in public. We were crazy.

Unlike this Maserati without a back seat, my car in law school had one long vinyl row. The number of times we crawled back there, too far from home to wait, too full of each other to care who might peer in, was a lot.

I want to touch his face, feel the line of his jaw. I give in, letting my fingers revisit all the places that once had been mine.

My thoughts get tangled between the present and the past. One time in my old car, he set the passenger seat back and pulled me on top of him. We were parked in the student lot at UC Berkeley, and people passed every few minutes.

"Mack," I said. "This is crazy, even for us."

"Leave your clothes on. Nobody's going to see."

He reached low, slid my panties down my legs, and spread my skirt over us.

I felt between us for the buckle to his jeans. "I can't believe we're doing this."

By then, I was on the pill, so we had a lot less fuss. I pulled him, hot and hard, out of his boxers and situated myself over him.

"Mack Squared, you are one crazy man. I didn't even lose a bet for this one."

"I'll take it as credit against your next loss," he said, his voice hitching as I lowered down on him.

He held my hips, moving me over him. I braced my

knees on the seat, glad now for such a boat of a car with plenty of room. I clutched the headrest, realizing I had real leverage to hang on to here, unlike the loose sheets of the bed.

The grinding of my pelvis down on him made him absolutely mad. He groaned and slipped a hand beneath my shirt and under the bra, thumbing my nipple. "Work it, Rory," he said.

I didn't require any encouragement. I had all the power, pushing fiercely against him, the friction hot between us. The orgasm was easy, deep, and lasted so long, sizzling out in zigzags of electric heat.

I never wanted it to end. Mack throbbed inside of me, but I kept going, drawing out the rhythmic pulse, my whole body zinging with the intensity.

Mack waited, his hands on my waist, and when I finally opened my eyes, exhilarated and high on endorphins, he was smiling up at me.

I smacked his chest. "What?"

"You're the most beautiful creature ever to walk this planet."

Usually I would argue with him that, objectively, the average model was seventy times hotter than me. But in that moment, I glowed with the connection between us, the good sex, the comfort we had with each other. I lay flat on his chest. "Thank you." I kissed his nose.

In the Maserati, I realize my hand is inside Mack's shirt, flirting with the snap of his jeans. His mouth is on my neck, and the wide-necked shoulder of my sweater is falling over the swell of my breast, pushed up by the strapless bra.

What are we doing? Is this what I want?

Parts of my body are saying, *Hell yes, I do.*

I hover for a moment. Do we fall back into this? Here? Now? It would be classic Mackory.

But then a light flashes across the front windshield, illuminating us for a moment.

I jerk back from Mack. "Night security," I say quickly.

Mack lets out a long, slow breath and pulls away. "Right. We're not young law students anymore."

"I don't have any experience in criminal law."

Mack looks at me a moment, then bursts out laughing. "Rory, you haven't changed one bit."

"Neither have you, mister."

Mack clears his throat. "I didn't plan to make any moves."

"You didn't? Given our history?"

His laugh is throaty. "I'd say, given our history, I didn't plan on ever seeing you again."

Ouch. But I deserve it. I did walk away and not look back.

"What do we do?"

His frown is evident, even in the shadows. "I'm not sure anymore."

The silence hangs. The happy sounds of the pier filter in. It feels out of sync with who we are now, and who we once were.

"I should go," I say.

"Can I see you again?" Mack asks.

"Yes," I say before I can think twice about it.

"Good," he says. A wave of seriousness crosses his face.

I throw open the door, glad for the chill to cool my body. Before Mack can follow me, I've hopped into my car and fired up the engine.

Was this what I wanted? Back with Mack?

He's so different. So sentimental. Emotional.

It has to be the Santa gig.

I still haven't gotten to the bottom of that.

He only said he wanted *more*. But by all accounts, he was at the top of his game as the best sports agent in town. What more could he possibly want?

Something in the way he sits there in his car, waiting for me to leave the parking lot first, suggests that the thing he wants more of...is me.

10

MACK

I spend Sunday morning searching the Internet for the right place to take Rory next. It comes time to meet my friend Henry to watch football, so I give up the search for the moment and head to the private sports bar where we generally meet.

Everyone here knows me. The general public can't get in, so this is where I take both my current and potential athlete clients while I'm wooing them.

Walking in is a lot like that old TV show *Cheers*. When the door opens, everyone turns to see who's come in, and most of the time, a big cheer goes up.

Sure enough, as I step inside, quite a few patrons call out my name. I wait for my eyes to adjust from the bright, sunshiny afternoon. The dim interior is lit by the double row of big screens lining the walls. Every sport is on.

There's a lot of footballers, all retired, of course, since it's Sunday in December, prime pigskin season. In fact, it looks like the Rams are having a bit of a reunion as the current team plays Dallas.

I lift my arm in greeting and wander the tables until I spot Henry. He already texted me to say he saved us a table.

We're exactly the same age, but the trajectory of our lives has been vastly different. Henry's gone domestic, married with two kids. It shows in his dad jeans, his sneakers. He's prematurely bald, so he buzzes his hair short to hide the receding hairline.

"Hey, Mack," he says, shoving a menu at me. "I already ordered us a pile of nachos."

"Thanks." I drag out the chair and plunk down across from him. The various television sets blare at us in surround sound. You can only start to pull out the audio of the one you want to hear if you read the closed captions.

"You look hella distracted," Henry says. "Did that gymnast not sign?"

"She did."

"Huh. You look like someone poked a hole in your kiddie pool."

"Been a week."

A tiny waitress with a disproportionate amount of cleavage sidles up. "Your usual, Mack?" she asks.

I nod.

Henry raises his eyebrows as she bounces off. "I know something's on your mind. It's never a woman with you, so which client is it?"

I could make something up. Say some athlete is causing trouble. But I don't. This is Henry, one of my best friends. "Actually, it's Rory Sheffield."

Henry smacks his hand on the table. "What the hell, Mack? Why are you even speaking her name?"

I watch his face carefully as I ask, "Did you know she was back in L.A.? Been back for four damn years."

Henry's good at hiding his thoughts, being a trial lawyer, but not that good. His eyes shift down before meeting mine again.

"I knew it," I say. "Did everybody know she was back in L.A. but me?"

Henry fiddles with his napkin. "To be honest, we all assumed you knew and were avoiding the topic."

"Who all is *we*?"

"The poker group. Jenessa. All the old guard."

"Nobody said anything for four damn years?" I can't believe it.

"Like I said, we assumed it was a sore subject. It's not like we see her either. She's holed up in her corporate law tower."

My drink arrives—scotch, neat—and I toss back half of it in a single gulp. The heavy glass hits the table with a thunk. "Well, I went out with her last night."

This makes Henry sit up straight in his chair. "Seriously? What the hell?"

"She showed up in the Santa line."

"She has a kid?"

"No. She was checking me out."

Henry shakes his head. "She has a lot of nerve just showing up."

I don't know quite how to explain to Henry how I feel about this. My actions don't make a lot of sense. I pretend to study the TV over our heads.

When Rory left after graduation, it caused a rift in our friend group. They all knew I planned to follow her. For a while, I let them think I was the asshole for not leaving. Henry was first to figure it out. And once word of Rory's request that I not go with her made its way around, especially since she quit reaching out to the others, they were all Team Mack.

Not that I wanted this to happen. A breakup is a breakup. There was no need to take sides. Nobody cheated. Nobody broke promises. We went our separate ways. But it didn't matter anyhow. None of us heard from her. She put up no defense for her actions. So I kept the friends.

"I know you're not that into the Chevy commercial," Henry says.

He's right. The game isn't even on.

"I'm going to see her again."

Henry runs the back of his hand over his scruffy cheek. "What for? To torture yourself?"

"We work. We always did, and we do now."

He lifts his beer. "Well, here's to overcoming the past. Good luck, my friend."

I clink my glass against his bottle.

I figure, given the circumstances, that asking Henry's advice on where to take Rory next would not go over well. But at halftime, he surprises me by saying, "Does Rory like football?"

I dig around the half-depleted plate of nachos for a

chip that isn't soggy. "I don't even know. I wasn't a sports agent when we were dating. And after that, who could tell?"

"It seems to me that if you're trying to impress someone like her, you should use what you've got."

I laugh. "What do you know about what I've got?"

"I don't mean *that*. I'm assuming that's not up for debate. You guys were like two rabbits in a meadow. I mean events. Big ones. Primo seats. You can get into anything."

He's right. But I can't imagine uptight Rory eating a hot dog at SoFi Stadium in her designer outfits.

Henry tilts his head toward a screen in the corner. A girl is flipping along a blue mat. "Don't all women love gymnastics?"

"I never say 'all women' about anything, not if I want my dick intact."

Henry grunts. "True. But you have some gymnastics people, right? Is there anything happening locally?"

"Maybe." I click through the calendar my assistant keeps for all the sporting events my clients are engaged in each day. Generally, she will formulate a generic message about their performance for me to pass on, and I will personalize it.

Today is busy with football, of course, but then I notice something else. An ice show. One of my former gymnasts switched to skating. There's an exhibition tonight in San Diego. It's a bit of a drive, but that makes for quality talk time. Rory and I seem to need that.

I dash off a quick message to Rory with the link to

the show. *One of my clients is performing tonight. Interested? She's good.*

Henry catches me staring at my phone. "Figure something out?"

"Ice skating."

"Now that's a slam dunk if I ever heard one."

I'm practically holding my breath waiting for a response. Henry notices. Of course he does.

Finally, I get a reply. *Never seen live ice skating.*

Too far to both drive. It's in San Diego. Should I pick you up?

There's another hesitation, and I wonder what she's thinking. Does she want to avoid being trapped with me again? A tendril of doubt trickles through me. This woman nearly killed me ten years ago. What am I doing? How much punishment do I need?

But when she replies, *Okay,* followed by an address, the way my chest expands in relief and anticipation tells me all I need to know.

I'll take whatever Rory dishes out. And like it.

11

RORY

I'M GLAD I CAME.

I might have felt some hesitation about seeing Mack again. We were so all over the place last night. But I've never gotten a chance to watch ice skating live.

Growing up, the Olympics were an enigma. They were always in some far-off place where travel plans had to be made years in advance. But we always watched them.

Mom wasn't much on leisure activities, but the Olympics were different. "This is where you see what it takes to be the best at something," she told me.

So it was a huge event. We'd map out the nights and weekends, which events to watch, what to eat, down to the bathroom breaks. We had lessons on judging, on how points were scored. Mom would point out which events had elements of subjectivity and which were purely objective.

And we loved the ice skating.

It's one of my few truly positive memories of childhood.

And now, here we are. It's not the Olympics, but it feels the same.

The arena is big. The very idea of building an ice rink where there would normally be a concert stage never even occurred to me.

Our seats are incredible—of course they are. Mack would settle for nothing less. It's chilly so close to the ice, but Mack warned me to bring a sweater. In the breaks between events, he tells me about Gemma, who is up in the next round.

"When did she start skating?" I ask.

"As soon as she could walk, as she tells it. That's common in the Northeast. She got serious about gymnastics around age six. But when she didn't qualify for the Olympics in gymnastics, she retired. She felt she was aging out and couldn't push any more than she was."

"At twenty-three?" I'm incredulous.

"It's a sport for the young, at least in the U.S. It's not as bad as it used to be. The minimum age to compete was fourteen for a long time. It's sixteen now."

"Poor thing. All that work."

"She loves skating more. I think she's happier."

She certainly looks it, gliding onto the rink to take the spotlight in the center.

I've seen some fantastic performances today, but I've been itching to see what it is about Gemma that made Mack sign her.

The music begins, flowing and melancholy. Gemma

moves fluidly around the oval, arms outstretched, eyes closed. She bends, arms fluttering, and I can feel her despair. I wonder what she thinks about to portray heartbreak so well.

The tempo speeds up, and she flashes across the rink, jumping, twirling, spinning in the air. The crowd cheers.

Then, just as quickly, she's back to the lament, lost, reaching for something slightly beyond her grasp.

There's no one else like her on the ice, not today. I grip the rail in front of us. Her face is expressive, skates weaving in and out as if she can't find what she's lost. Her ice-blue skirt flutters behind her as she speeds up again, anxious, desperate, until she whirls into a wild spin.

It goes on and on and on, defying the laws of motion, her body a blur. I don't know how she can keep going, how she doesn't fly apart. But she plants her skate and stills, arms up, and the crowd is on its feet.

But there is more. She's figuring out how to be, how to exist without the thing she's seeking. She stops looking, holding her arms around her waist. She must be enough on her own.

I'm crying. I hate that. I never cry. I pretend to straighten my hair and quickly dash the tears away. When she hits her final pose, I leap up again, clapping and screaming and cheering.

Mack stands next to me. He seems bemused, a half-smile on his face.

People toss flowers onto the ice, and Gemma glides along, picking them up easily. I wonder where they got those flowers. I wish I had some to throw. She spots Mack and waves.

When I sit down, Mack says, "I see Gemma has a new fan."

"Totally. You can take me anywhere she's performing."

"Would you like to meet her?"

My heart catches. "Of course I would."

"There will be three more in this round, then a break. We can go back then."

I can barely sit still. What would Mom say? I pull out my phone to text her, but then stop myself. Mom and I don't text casually. I tuck the phone away.

The other competitors are good, but nothing like Gemma. When more skaters glide onto the ice for a warmup during the break, Mack stands. "Let's go back. Say hello."

I feel inexplicably shy, as if I will botch the introduction. We head to the aisle to climb the stairs. When we get to the arena level, I quickly move in beside him. "We should bring some flowers or something. I can't meet her empty-handed!"

"Of course." He turns us the other direction, toward a flower cart. "Pick anything you like."

I choose perfect pink roses with red tips. Mack pays for them and takes my hand as we slip down a side hall. A guard waits at the end.

"Mack McAllister," Mack says. "For Gemma King."

The man pulls a clipboard off the wall and takes his time flipping through it. "All right. Next time, have a badge."

Mack and I grin at each other like kids skipping school as we continue along a hallway that angles down like a ramp. Soon we hear noise ahead, people pushing racks of costumes, competitors with bags talking earnestly to coaches.

"This way," Mack says, and I follow him through the crowd to a set of double doors thrown open wide. Inside is a makeshift dressing room, tables set up, chairs everywhere. Skaters examine themselves in mirrors, tap on phones, or sit and wait. I recognize several from the earlier rounds.

"You were so good," I tell a couple in midnight-blue outfits. "And you too," I say to a woman in a red costume.

They nod in acknowledgment.

"There she is," Mack says, pulling me to the far corner.

Gemma still wears her ice-blue dress. She's adjusting her laces, listening to a fierce-looking woman talk in loud, rapid bursts.

She sees us and smiles. "Mack! You're here!" She jumps up to give him a hug. "What did you think?"

The other woman rolls her eyes and plunks onto the wood bench.

Mack squeezes Gemma. "You were superb. Everyone is going to be talking about you after the medal ceremony."

I watch him envelop the tiny woman in his arms with a twinge of jealousy. How easy it must be to know Mack without the baggage of a difficult past. I wonder if he's ever dated a client, if that's even allowed.

Gemma releases him and peers at me. "Are you going to introduce me?"

Mack takes my hand. "Gemma, this is Rory Sheffield. She's a corporate lawyer who makes her opponents quake in their boots."

Now *that's* an introduction.

"She's also your biggest fan," he adds.

"Oh!" Gemma's smile is bright. "I can use those now that I've switched teams, as it were."

I pass her the flowers. "Nobody was as good as you," I say. "Not even close."

"Oh!" she says again. "That's some praise!" Her cheeks brighten. She turns to Mack. "I like her!"

"How are you holding up?" Mack asks.

Gemma's eyes glimmer, and I realize she's having a hard time. I can't even imagine it. She is so good.

"I miss my old friends. But it seems that once you leave the lifestyle, you're out of the circles." She bites her lip, and suddenly I completely see where the tragedy of her performance comes from. She's been abandoned by her gymnast friends now that she skates.

"Did you make any headway on a doubles partner?" he asks.

She shakes her head. "I'm hoping if I do well tonight, I might drum up more interest."

"It'll come," Mack assures her.

Gemma wipes a tear away. "I hope so. It's not easy, starting over."

"You will shine," Mack says. "You're terrific. Everyone will want to skate with you."

Gemma gives him a nod, but her eyes belie her fear.

He squeezes her wrist. "I'll let your coach get back to her assessment," he says. "Be good to my star skater," he says to the coach.

The woman scarcely acknowledges him. Gemma sits back down, and the stream of commentary continues.

As we dodge skaters and benches and racks to return to the hall, I say, "You're good with your clients."

"That's part of the job," Mack says. "She won't be lonely for long. It's an adjustment. Skaters don't have the same proximity that gymnastics teams do. There are no built-in best friends. But she'll make them. They'll want to know her."

"I will be her first big fan."

Mack grins at me, and I realize that we can have a great time, even now.

12

MACK

I'M INCREDIBLY PLEASED ABOUT HOW THE NIGHT HAS gone as we drive from San Diego back to L.A. Rory's face is lit by the glow of her phone as she orders "Team Gemma" shirts from some online shop for next time. She's getting extras so she can recruit super fans.

I forgot how she can throw herself into a project. It's beautiful to watch.

"So when is her next competition?" Rory asks. "I want to make sure I get these in time."

"I'll text it to you. It's not until January, although she might have a Christmas exhibition."

"Oh, but you might be working. We'll be getting into the holiday party zone soon."

"I'm not taking any private gigs. Well, other than a couple of hospitals."

She sets her phone down. "You're going to be Santa in some hospitals?"

The highway lights flash by as I focus on the road.

"In Santa School they suggest you balance the paid gigs with volunteering."

"Isn't that going to be hard with two jobs already?"

I glance over at her. I can barely make out her features in the dark. "I like to think that the hard things make us stronger."

She looks out the window then. I didn't intend to get all serious, or to reference our breakup again. Time to lighten the mood.

"What did Darth Vader say when Santa asked him how he knew what was under the Christmas tree?"

"Oh boy." She sounds skeptical that I can deliver on this.

"I feel your presents."

I can't see her expression, but there's a burst of air, like she's holding back a snort. "Do you memorize these?"

"What? You don't think I'm a natural comedian?"

"Did you pick up this skill since law school?"

It feels good to laugh with her. "Nah. Just recently. I wanted to be able to make the kids giggle. Makes for good pictures."

"So I'm not the target market for your humor."

"I think you're the perfect test subject. If I can make serious, all-business Rory Sheffield laugh, then I can do it to anyone."

She chortles at that. "All true. I'm pretty immune to dad jokes, though."

"So when does a joke become a dad joke?"

"When nobody laughs anymore?"

"Nice one. But it's when the punch line becomes a-parent."

"Oh no, you didn't." She presses the back of her hand to her mouth.

"I guess since I tell so many dad jokes without having any kids of my own, that makes me a *faux pas*."

She waves her arm at me. "You have to stop it!"

I spot a sign for a scenic overlook ahead and decide to make a stop. As I slow down on the approach, I say, "Did you know the ocean never says goodbye?"

She sobers at that. We've returned to farewells. "What does it say instead?"

"It just waves."

I exit the freeway and pull into the pair of parking spots at the overlook. There's no one else there. A concrete barrier creates a sturdy point where the white foam of the sea breaks against the cliff on either side.

"Let's take a peek," I say.

The roar is enormous as we come together in front of the car and lean against the concrete wall. The moon is almost full, sending a wavering white line of light along the surface of the water.

There might be no one else in the world. The exit goes only here, then back to the highway. On either side are cliffs covered in rock and scrub brush. The waves are relentless, crashing one after the other, an incessant beat of the ocean.

"A place like this makes you feel powerless," Rory says. "Insignificant and small."

"It's humbling." I shift closer so that our bodies connect.

She tugs her sweater around her. "I missed this when I was in Boston. Sometimes I swore the West Coast was calling to me to come back."

"Is that why you returned to California?"

"Partly. My mom's here, too. And my grandparents."

"Do you see them more than you did back then? I only remember you going back for Christmas."

"Still just Christmas."

"I never did meet your mom." It didn't bother me in the least during those two years that Rory never took me to see her family. I never took her to see mine either. We had a tacit understanding that such a meeting wasn't important to us. Escaping a difficult home life was one of the things that formed our bond.

"What do you do on holidays these days?" she asks. "We always spent them together."

"Volunteer, mostly. I did have Thanksgiving dinner with Henry a couple of weeks ago."

"Does he have kids?"

"Oh, yes, two real ankle biters."

She shoves her shoulder against mine. "Santa can't say that."

"I say it with all the love in my heart."

We stare out at the water. The power of the crashes seems to diminish as we stand there, even though the force of the waves is the same. It gets ordinary, expected, like hard things tend to do. It becomes your new normal.

"What did you miss the most when you struck out to Boston?" I don't know why I ask this. It's not like Rory is going to say, "You." It's almost as though I'm needling the wound.

But her answer surprises me. "Sex."

I almost choke on my reaction. "What? Really?"

She shrugs. "Sure. You and I had this longstanding relationship built on wild attraction and perfectly matched sex drives. I couldn't re-create that out of nothing."

I'm not sure I want to hear any more about her attempts to get crazy with some other man. But before I can interject, she says, "I didn't even bother."

I let out a sigh. But then I catch myself. For how long? I itch to know the answer. I said those awful things on the Ferris wheel, which made her scoot away from me and start the whole panic attack. What she did without me was none of my business.

But damn it if I was going to let her forget what it was like.

As if nature itself has heard my thoughts, the wind picks up, and a light mist from the spray crosses our bodies. "This is wild!" Rory shouts.

I turn her toward me to shield her, and before either of us can think twice about it, we're interlocked in a frenzied kiss that rivals the crash of the sea.

13

RORY

Something about this spot has put me over the edge.

I cling to Mack, wild with his kiss. Our mouths devour each other—lips, jaw, neck. I snake my arms inside his jacket, reveling in his warmth, the hard, muscled plane of his chest and flat belly.

His need for me is clear as our bodies press together. It's been so long. So terribly, achingly long. Once again, I don't confess to Mack the truth about my sexual history. I was a virgin the first time with him. And since then, no man I've dated has come close, not in kisses, not in touch. So I've never turned my body over to anyone else.

It didn't feel worth it.

But I'm back where I used to be, lost in the fervor of Mack. He tugs my silk shirt from the waist of my skirt, sliding his hands along my skin.

He reaches behind my back to release the bra, and his palms cup me as I arch for him, warm and naked.

I'm not shy with him. We were never reluctant or coy. We played no games when it came to this. I unfasten his tailored dress pants and jerk down the zipper. Then he's in my hands as well, swollen and long and throbbing. I've missed everything about this. The taste, the feel, the sense that I've lost myself in a tempest.

The wind and the crash of the waves drive my frenzy. Mack groans against my mouth. "Rory."

"Yes," I tell him. "Like we used to. Right here."

He lifts me to sit on the wide ledge of the concrete barrier. The ocean crashes at my back, the mist soaking my hair.

But I'm not cold, not in the least. I'm hot and thrilled and more ready for this than anything that's happened to me in ten long, terrible years. I forgot how intoxicating this is, how passionate and wild.

Mack jerks down my panties and, when they catch on my boots, rips them away. He spreads my knees, and his fingers are between my legs, his thumb circling my aching clit. I try to control myself, not give away how long it's been. But I'm overwrought, wound too tightly. The orgasm begins so fast and so hard that its will is stronger than mine.

I cry out directly in Mack's ear, and he holds me close against his chest, cupping me as the pulsing goes on and on. I'm crying, which never happened before, and I'm glad, so glad for the wind and the mist and the dark. I'm not emotional, was never emotional. Why has this act brought me to tears?

I bite down on my lip to make it stop and reach for

Mack. "I want it now," I tell him. "Don't hold anything back."

He knows what I mean. He shoves my legs even farther apart, dragging me forward on the ledge so that my skirt snags on the concrete. I hear another rip, a seam giving way as he jerks me toward him, his aim perfect, and my body receives him like the perfect fit of a puzzle piece.

I drape my arms around his neck, hanging on as he grips my hips, slamming his body against mine. It's fierce and powerful and makes my head go light. We're fitted together as if merging as one, the length of him creating the connection that makes us whole. My thighs ache, but the hunger is ravenous. I need him as deep as we can go.

We reach that space where the friction of his body and mine sends lightning bolts of crazed pleasure through my belly and hips. I tilt up to him, ignoring the strain, wanting all of it, to feel everything I've missed.

I let go and brace myself on my hands, my sweater falling away, the wet silk clinging to my body. Mack is like a beast now, shoving the shirt aside, exposing me to the wind and mist and fury of the cliff side.

The coil I've held so tightly inside me begins to unfurl like a tornado dropping from the sky. Mack holds me, plunging in, out, also meeting his edge.

For a second, everything goes silent, inside and out, like the dead calm before an explosive blast. I can almost see us as if I'm a bystander, my clothes peeled away, naked skin exposed to the mist. I'm held by Mack's strong arms, his hand beneath me, my knees on either side of his body.

Time stops for a moment. The waves cease to crash. The sky is dark, the stars dazzling. The storm awaits, holding this scene in place for me to examine, to feel completely, to absorb into my soul.

Then everything unleashes at once. The orgasm, the emotion, the fear, the regret. Even as my body contracts around him, I can't help but scream into the crash of the waves. Mack calls out, "Rory," in a primal yell as he spills into me, arms straining, the cords on his neck standing out.

I want to keep yelling until I'm hoarse, until I can drown out all the mistakes I made, rewind time, make things right. But Mack falls over me, his forehead on my shoulder. I clasp his head and bring his face up to look at me.

He seems tortured, as if this was exactly what he sought to avoid, but I brought him down a second time. The pain is there, as if he's sure he will lose me once more.

"I'm here, Mack. I'm back. We're back."

He kisses my shoulder, my neck, my breasts. He wants to touch it all, taste it all, and I let him have his reunion with my body. Every place his mouth touches sizzles in the mist. I'm electrically alive, all the reserve I've held blasted away.

At last he steps back so I can drop my feet to the ground. My skirt falls uselessly to my ankles. My panties have melted into the mud. My shirt no longer closes. I have to laugh.

"Mack McAllister, you are a beast."

He laughs, pulling my long sweater around me and tying it closed. It falls to my thighs, so it works as a modest cover-up. "You're so sexy like this that I'll probably do it a second time before we get home."

And he's not lying. We're not even to the outskirts of Los Angeles when he reaches over and shoves the damp sweater aside to slip his fingers inside me.

I'm aching and sore already, but I don't mind. I kick the seat back, spread my knees, and go along for the ride.

14

MACK

20 Days to Christmas

Once we turn on the faucet, there is no shutting it off.

I spend the night at Rory's house. We get very little sleep. It's like old times all over again. Nonstop itches that need to be scratched.

I don't have office hours, so I can do as I please. But Rory misses her eight a.m. meeting. While she talks to her assistant, trying to reschedule, my mouth is quite occupied. At one point she has to physically hold my head away to focus on the conversation. It's beautiful.

We finally separate for the day, Rory encouraging me to forage in the kitchen for something to eat and dashing out the door. It's a familiar circumstance from when we lived together, constantly on the run.

Now that she's gone, Sir Winston follows me around with suspicion. He's a sixty-pound black lab who thinks he's a lap dog. Every time Rory sat down, he tried to squish his way on top of her.

Which is why we started in the shower last night.

But he doesn't sleep on her bed, settling in his own big sheepskin enclosure emblazoned with his name. So we didn't have company there.

He gives me the stink-eye as I look around the kitchen.

"You'll have to get used to me, I think," I tell him.

Rory's kitchen looks like a magazine spread, all gleaming marble countertops with bright teal accessories. I spot a cookie jar labeled "Sir Winston" and open the top. Dog biscuits. I know the way to a canine's heart.

I bend down to feed one to him. He snatches it from my hand and walks several steps away, watching me with disdain.

"I get it," I say. "She was all yours until I came along."

I open her fridge. Every fruit and vegetable has its own clear container. Her lunches are neatly prepacked in a row. Maybe her dinners, too. There's a lot. Their teal lids match the rest of the place.

I'm almost afraid to touch anything. I'll wreck her system.

But she did make double the coffee, so I open the cabinet for a mug and fill it from the gleaming steel percolator on a tray with creamer and sugar jars marked in teal script.

Rory wasn't anything like this when we lived together. Towels on the floor, half-eaten leftovers in the fridge. It wasn't a pigsty—we kept the basics clean—but our place was definitely cluttered and disorganized.

I sit on a stool at the bar and contemplate this change. Too much time on her hands? A bevy of house-keeping staff? Has she gotten strait-laced with her home life, meticulous like her studies used to be?

I bet that's it. Outside of the structure of classwork and scheduled lectures, she had to create her own systems of organization. And she hadn't known where to stop.

I sip the coffee. Nothing about this house looks lived in, other than the occasional dog toy lying about. I don't want to snoop, but I do walk around, taking in the art she's bought and the books on her shelves. No surprises there.

I rinse the mug in the sink and pad back upstairs to gather my clothes. Rory slung them over the towel bar to dry. They stand out against the pale green color palette.

I wonder what she will think of my place, all black leather and sports memorabilia. It's not half as neat, although my housekeeper Jillian manages to keep it mostly straight.

I decide to take a shower there before I leave, breathing in the scent of Rory's body wash and sham-poo. I'll probably cover it with aftershave before I put on the Santa suit this afternoon, but for now, I'm content to keep Rory on my skin.

Sir Winston waits on the bath mat when I come out. He sniffs the air, then must decide I'm okay because he stays by my side as I get dressed.

"You're a good dog," I tell him, scratching his chin.

His tail wags. Apparently we can be friends.

"If only figuring out your Rory was as easy," I tell him.

He lets out a little snort.

"Exactly."

I give him another biscuit on my way out, the first bit of concern starting to hit me with the bright morning sun. One thing about rekindling an old flame is that it burns really hot, really fast. We're proof of that.

But I don't know where this is going. It could be a one-off. It's not like we made a love connection. Just a collision of body parts.

I'll have to stay on guard, or I might find myself living that torturous period without her all over again.

15

RORY

I'm late. I'm never late.

Jerome lifts his perfectly arched eyebrows at me as I fly by his desk, already five minutes past the start of my second meeting of the day. I missed the first one completely, dragged back beneath the sheets when my alarm went off.

God almighty, Mack is going to kill me. I lost count of orgasms around five. I'm out one skirt and one pair of panties. I have a scrape on my thigh from the concrete overlook, and one bruise on my elbow from the shower. And in a few hours, it's all going to catch up to me, every muscle sore as hell, a level of exhaustion I haven't known since exam weeks. The crash is coming.

And I can't wait to do it all over again.

I drop my bag behind my desk. Jerome swoops in. "Martin Bellevue is in the conference room. Alaina is already going over the briefs as if it's standard procedure for her to start without you." He passes me a folder and a cup of coffee. "You have so damn much to tell me when this is over."

"I will." I move around him and hurry to the conference room, slowing down only when I'm visible through the glass wall.

Alaina pauses her PowerPoint presentation as I open the door. "And here she is."

"Martin, so good to see you." I set down my coffee and reach out to shake his hand. "Looks like I'm a bit early. Alaina, you go right ahead and finish out."

I have the best staff. The. Best. Alaina doesn't miss a beat, continuing with the information about the trademark issues we've encountered for Martin's line of athletic wear and our proposed solutions. I shake Mack loose from my thoughts and focus in. I have a job to do.

The meeting runs long, and I have zero break until the next one. It's lunch before I can sit at my desk and let the weekend catch up with me.

Jerome enters with his sandwich and plunks down on the sofa in the corner. "Break out your power lunch and tell me everything," he says.

I pull up my calendar. I have three more meetings this afternoon, all with difficult problems to work through. This will be my only moment of downtime.

"Give me a sec," I say. "Today is brutal."

"Indeed. Jacobson was none too happy to get pushed back."

"I'm sorry about that." Damn it. I have to get myself together.

I should text Mack, but my annoyance at my lack of self-control and its impact on my clients makes me leave my phone in my drawer. He might have texted me this morning. I don't know. I'll deal with that if I have time before my one o'clock.

I head to the mini-fridge hidden in my cabinets and extract my spinach salad, then situate myself in the armchair next to the sofa. "So I went out with him."

"Girl, I could have told you that from the moment you got on the phone. First, you weren't here ahead of me. Second, you missed the first meeting in the history of your history."

"Did any of the other partners catch wind of it?" I ask, although I'm not sure I want to know.

"Of course not. I handled it myself."

I let out a sigh.

Jerome leans toward me. "So he was with you this morning. Making you late."

I pop the teal lid off my salad container. "He was."

"You were on fire when you got here this morning, but now you look like you're putting yourself on a walk of shame. Did you have a good time?"

"Well, yeah." I stuff a forkful of spinach in my mouth. The pomegranate dressing is to die for. I melt back into the chair.

"So, set an early alarm next time. No harm, no foul."

"Tell that to Jacobson."

"His dumb ol' patent is never getting approved, and he should know it."

"He keeps paying us to try."

"Definition of insanity, if you ask me."

"There's always another angle to submit."

"Speaking of angles, how many did our good man Mack try on you?"

I shake my head. Jerome has always tried to have this level of conversation with me, but I've never taken the bait. Why is Mack different?

Right—I've never been late before.

"Many," I say. "We were wild in law school, and apparently nothing has changed."

Jerome sighs. "I need an injection of new blood in my circle," he says. "I want to feel what you're feeling."

"Probably not in a few hours." I show him my elbow bruise. "Everything's going to hurt."

"The best type of injuries," he says. "And color me impressed."

We eat for a bit, but I can tell by Jerome's foot shake that he has more to say. "Out with it."

"I get the feeling this isn't a love match," he says. "Are you just playing around?"

"It's been one weekend," I say. "Nobody is in love after two days."

"Not sure about that." He turns the remaining half of his sandwich over in his hands. "There were all the years before, right?"

"Mack and I have a hefty respect for each other's intellects and career paths, and we have a good time in bed. Why mess that up with emotion?"

"Why, indeed?"

"You have, what, four relationships right now? Are you in love with all of them?"

Jerome takes a bite of his bread. "I'm in love with carbs, that's for sure."

"Hey, don't dodge. You've been asking me the tough questions."

"I know. I guess I'm in love with each of them in their own way."

"And if any one of them left you—"

"Oh, I'd be devastated. No, no, no."

I don't tell him I wasn't devastated to leave Mack. Inconvenienced, for sure. It turned out he was more irreplaceable than I thought he'd be. But it's unlikely to be any different this time around. We don't even live together.

And he asked me if I was *more* of what I used to be when we were together before.

I think I must be. Because I am definitely *more* determined not to let my personal life impact my career.

16

MACK

I FEEL BAD ABOUT RORY MISSING HER MEETING. I TELL her so in a text, but I don't hear back until late in my afternoon shift, when I take my only fifteen-minute break.

Finally. I was beginning to wonder if we were over as soon as we started.

I read it with the eagerness of a preteen boy.

Today's been brutal. Did you find some breakfast?

It's not exactly what I was looking for from Rory, but after seeing her place, I know she's gone further down the rabbit hole of trying to orchestrate the perfect life than before.

I say what she might expect me to say.

My early morning snack held me over pretty well.

Mack!

When do I get to feast on you again?

It must work, because her next text reads, *I thought I might need some recovery time, but it turns out you're both the illness and the cure.*

This makes me smile bigger than a five-year-old on Christmas morning.

I want to suggest tonight, but to do that, I'd have to cancel my late night with the footballers on my list, the ones no longer playing. They watch the Monday games and talk trash about the current stars. We do this every few weeks, and I hit them up with opportunities I've seen for sponsorships and the like.

It won't end until well after midnight, and I did already keep Rory up too much last night. There's no gap either, not between Santa hours, home, cleanup, and racing across town.

I decide this is too much for texting, so I make a quick call.

She answers on the first ring. "Hey, Mack."

"Are you home?"

"Just got in."

I glance at the clock on the wall. "You worked late."

"It was a meeting-filled day, so I had to play catch-up." She yawns.

"Tired?"

"I didn't get much sleep last night for some reason." I can almost see her smile.

"I would very much like to keep you up all night again soon."

"You will have to let me recover."

I bet she does. "Not a problem. I'm working like mad anyway. I'll be Santa Monday through Thursday all the way to close this week."

"I thought you were the B Santa."

"The other Santa has some private gigs this week, so I got all the shifts."

"How do you manage in that suit all day?" she asks.

"It has a cooling vest."

"Nice. And a pillow, I guess? You looked rather plump the time I saw you."

"It's special padding that goes under the jacket. I'm not a proper Santa without all my accessories."

"So it sounds like Friday before we'll get together."

I hate to admit it, but she's probably right. "Friday seems so far away."

She laughs. "You sound like a teenage boy."

"I *feel* like a teenage boy."

"You were recycling like a teenage boy."

"You bring out the best in me."

"Mmm."

I spot curled elf shoes coming down the stairs to the green room. It's Steve, tonight's Santa handler. We're in a level underneath the mall, directly below the stage on the main concourse. The secret stairs allow Santa, or whatever act is performing, to reach the stage without wandering the mall first.

"Time for me to get back out there," I say.

"All right, Mack. Have fun."

I set the phone in my secure locker and chug a glass of water. It's go-time for Santa again.

"It will get crazier and crazier all the way to Christmas Eve," Steve says. He bends down to straighten his striped tights.

He doesn't love the gig. At least twice a day he mutters, "Serves me right for getting a degree in fashion design." His work in costuming dried up, and he ended up wearing the very elf suit he designed to pay rent.

"I guess we better get back in there, then," I say.

And up the stairs we go.

Monday and Tuesday are a blur of Santa sessions.

On Wednesday, Steve has to leave early, so my handler is Theo, who is not quite as adept at managing the flow.

I'm already four hours in without a break but manage to keep it going. I might have to start chugging Red Bull.

A mom holding a baby leads a small girl in pigtails up to me.

"What's your name?" I ask her.

"Amelia." She stands by my knee and gazes up at me with solemn eyes. "Are you the real Santa?"

I get this about a thousand times a day. "I can definitely listen to what you want for Christmas."

This is enough for her. It usually is for the preschoolers. She climbs up onto the sofa to sit beside me.

Mom lowers the baby into my arms. I'm well practiced. Long before the Santa gig, before Rory and law school, I was a big brother tasked with taking care of the smallest of our brood. I can change a diaper in ten seconds flat. My younger brother Simon used to time me.

"You have to hold her head up more," Amelia says,

getting on her knees so she can adjust her baby sister's position.

Mom steps back so the pictures can begin.

"Do I have it right now?" I ask her.

"It's good enough," Amelia says. "She's not crying. I cried when I saw you last year. Sowwy."

"It's okay. New things are scary."

She peers up at me. "Do you ever cry?"

"Sometimes."

"What about?"

That's a loaded question. "Rudolph accidentally kicked me in the shin the other day. That made me cry."

She giggles. "Santa, you're silly."

"I am pretty silly. Do you know what you want for Christmas?"

She nods. "I want Mama to stop holding the baby so much."

I glance up at the mom, who has lowered her phone.

"Babies need to be held a lot," I say. "You got held a lot when you were a baby."

"Oh, I was never a baby," Amelia says. "I've always been a big girl."

"I believe you," I say. "What if you had your own baby to hold? Could you sit next to your mama and hold your baby while she holds hers?"

She seems to consider this idea, her head tilted. "Would it poop? I don't like it when the baby poops."

I chuckle. "No, your baby doesn't have to poop."

She holds out her hand like a used car salesman. "Deal!"

I shake hers. "You want to smile at the camera for a picture?"

She nods. "Mom said if I took a pretty picture I could have ice cream."

"That sounds wonderful."

"Do you like ice cream?"

"I do."

I point toward Elf Jess, who shakes a teddy bear over the camera. Amelia turns and gives the big, cheesy smile common for kids her age. I shift the baby so she is more visible.

A couple of snaps, and they're down. If only they were all so easy to convince.

Mom takes the baby and whispers, "Thank you. I had no idea."

"No problem." It's common for kids to have requests that have nothing to do with toys. I try to roll with it.

There's a bit of a commotion at the start of the line. Theo is blocking someone, but she finally pushes through.

She's young, early twenties, wearing a seriously tiny skirt that exposes her midriff and a fur-lined red top that barely contains a heaping amount of cleavage.

The elves perk up. Theo shrugs.

"Hello," I say. "You decided to see Santa."

"I'm an Instagram influencer," she says. "I have over one million followers. Smile!" She holds a selfie stick with her phone and starts madly shooting.

Normally one of the handlers will gently suggest a visitor allow the official photographer to get some shots, but it's clear Jess has no intention of intervening.

The other elves seem mesmerized.

The woman shifts in my lap, kicking up a foot. Her white-trimmed red platform stilettos top an extremely long leg. She's really fast at getting her shots.

Theo seems content at letting her stay as long as she wants. When the woman lifts her skirt to reveal a fur-trimmed thong, Jess says, "That's enough," and races our way. The woman sees her coming and kisses my cheek.

"Thanks so much, big guy!" She squeezes my arm. "Oh, Santa's got guns!" She sizes me up again. "What's under that suit?"

"You got your shots," Jess says, gesturing for the side gate. "Let the kids have their turn."

The woman rolls her eyes at Jess but gets off my lap, hustling for the gate as if afraid they'll try to sell her a kiddie package of prints. She needn't worry. Jess didn't take a single shot.

I shake it off. Theo heads back to the gate for the next family. The clock over the escalator reads eight. One hour to close, although next week, the mall expands to holiday hours.

It's going to get even more intense.

17

RORY

18 Days to Christmas

I don't remember feeling this pent-up before.

I walk in crazy circles around my house, Sir Winston faithfully following along behind.

I'm like a lioness in a cage. Tense, coiled up, and about as feral.

I keep talking out loud to myself. "Rory, you are a full-grown professional woman who has been single for a decade. You're fine."

Sir Winston perks his ears at my tone. He's never seen me like this.

I have never seen me like this.

I glance at the clock for the thousandth time. Eight thirty. Mack will be done with his Santa shift in a half-hour.

It takes a half-hour to get to the mall.

"No, no. We said this weekend. I will wait until this weekend."

On one of the circles around my kitchen, I pick up my keys, jingling them.

Sir Winston trots beside me.

"What do you think, Winnie? Should I go?"

He gives a low whine at the mention of his name.

"Was that a yes or a no?"

Another uneasy whine.

I'm expecting an answer from my dog.

I stop cold. What am I doing?

Sir Winston sits on his haunches, then lifts his paw to pat against my knee.

I bend down to pet his head. "I should follow my gut here, right? That's what you'd do?"

He wags his tail. I get it. Be happy.

Right now, Mack makes me happy.

So I rush out to the garage and drive to Riverside Mall.

When I arrive, I sit in my car, my fingers hovering over the phone screen. I should text him. Let him know I've come. It's five minutes to nine. I made good time.

Except he'll still be with kids. He won't even get the text. I should get in there before the mall closes, though. The last thing I need is to be locked out.

With this new thought in mind, I dash out of the car and head toward the mall entrance.

As I hurtle through the door, I realize I'm acting like an addict needing a hit.

And the hit I need is Mack McAllister.

Oh, this is bad. So, so, so, so bad.

I slow down when I reach the main concourse. Mack holds a small boy in his lap. The child whispers something in his ear. For a moment, my heart squeezes.

"Knock it off," I tell my dumb body, and an elderly lady with an armful of packages shoots me a dirty look.

I have to stop saying this stuff out loud.

The line is short, with only two families left. The elf I ran into last week stands at the end of it, turning people away. Mack will get off on time. I'm not sure if I should approach him and be seen by them again. Or if I can wait for him to leave and then text him.

This was a bad idea.

I ride the escalator to the floor above. It looks down on the Santa set, where the little boy is hopping down. I can watch from the upper level without being seen.

But Mack must have some sixth sense about me. As the escalator moves me past him, he sees me and waves.

The elf doesn't even bother to look. Maybe Mack waves at passersby a lot. Maybe he doesn't even know it's me.

But then he motions for me to come back down.

I fight a few steps in the opposite direction, then realize that is ridiculous and ride to the top, then go down. By the time I'm passing him again, he has a baby and a tiny toddler in his lap. Neither child is talking age, so they are all looking forward as the weary photographer elf tries to get their attention for a photo.

By the time I'm down and near the set, the last family has come up. This one has three children, all very neat and beautifully dressed.

Mom arranges them around Mack, placing the

smallest one on his lap. They all smile perfectly for several shots. The mom calls them away, but Mack holds up his hand. He talks to each of them, nodding thoughtfully as they speak to him. Apparently harried moms who only want their picture will be usurped by a Santa who wants to make sure the children are heard.

My dumb heart skips a beat.

The all-American family heads to the photo cashier, and the main elf closes the gate that gives access to Santa. I hurry to the border fence surrounding the set. Mack sees me and strides over.

"Ho, ho, ho!" he says. "Hello, young lady. Do you have something you want Santa to do for you?"

I shake my head. "That's really dirty."

He leans close. "I'm hoping so."

My whole body starts to pulse. "How do I get you out of here?" I ask.

His eyebrows lift, visible even with all the white hair and glasses. "I think you should come to my secret hideaway."

Now we're talking. He walks me along the fence to the exit gate, where the last family is leaving after getting their photos. I wait for them to pass by, and Mack waves at them. "Merry Christmas!"

He holds the gate for me and says softly, "We'll wait a moment until the concourse is clear."

I glance around. A few shoppers walk the open areas even as the individual stores begin to lower their sliding metal doors to lock up. The photographer elf loads her camera equipment in a cabinet beneath the cash register, and the seller elf closes out the receipts.

The elf who tends the line watches me with the same suspicion I recall from last week. "I remember you," he says.

Mack turns to him. "Theo, this is Rory."

Theo crosses his arms. "You jumped in the line without a kid. Caused quite the stir."

"I did take a tumble." Coming here is starting to feel like the worst idea ever.

"I can handle things now," Mack says. "Are you working tomorrow?"

"No, just Steve. I'll be here Saturday for the madness."

"That's the A Santa."

Theo nods. "Benson has been the lead Santa here for a decade."

"He's a good one."

Theo takes off across the set and out through the gate. The photographer elf slides a bag over her shoulder. "See you tomorrow, Santa," she says.

Mack gives her a wave. "You good?" he asks the elf at the register.

"I'm good."

"Tomorrow, then!" He walks toward his sofa and gestures for me to follow.

We pass through a narrow entrance hidden by how the front facade of the set overlaps the back. We turn sharply behind the rear wall so we're surrounded by a powdery white mountain with a snowman on top. We can no longer see the main concourse, and even the upstairs is obscured by the curve of the set.

"The secret exit," Mack says, tapping his black boot

on the floor. It activates a mechanism that lifts a hidden door. He bends down to open it wide, and a set of stairs is illuminated below. "Follow me."

He starts down the stairs, pausing halfway down to watch me. The first few steps are unnerving, but then I can hold on to the floor, then a metal rail as we descend into a large, open room.

"This is a staging area for performers," Mack explains. "The regular acts like the student choirs and all don't use it, but anybody who might be spotted walking through the mall will come through the employees' entrance to this room."

"I had no idea this was down here." Of course, I'd never been to this mall before last week, either.

Mack tugs off his hat, revealing the white wig and beard combination. I move in to take a closer look. "I like yours better than the ones that are wild and curly."

"I was going for more of the silver fox effect." He takes my hand and lays it on his beard. "But give it a good tug."

I grasp a bit of the straight white hair and pull down. It doesn't budge. "That's good."

"It's a bit of a thing taking it off and on. It's all glued down."

"Can I help?"

His green eyes meet mine. "Yes."

"I assume you don't walk out of here as Santa."

"No, it's in my contract that I dress normally when I exit the building. Some of the Santas have real hair and beards, though. They can only change their outfits."

"I'm sure they don't want their mall Santa cutting someone off in the parking lot."

"Exactly."

Mack shrugs out of his Santa jacket, revealing a big stuffed tank top.

I can't resist pounding my hands on it. "Santa's belly."

"I think I get a hint of what it's like to be pregnant when I wear it." He turns to the side, and I have to laugh.

"You're more than nine months along, I think."

He reaches behind to unclasp the straps holding it on.

I take it from him. "That's a lot to lug around."

He nods. Now his chest is covered in a sporty-looking blue and black vest.

"What's that?" I ask.

"The cooling vest. It doesn't last the whole shift, but it helps." He unzips the front and shrugs it off as well. Beneath that is a tight cotton T-shirt that clings to his chest and biceps. I feel the heat as I watch him pack the cooling vest and the belly in a duffel bag. I remember clutching those arms on the cliff.

I take Mack's Santa jacket and put it on. "It's warm," I say, petting the velvety fur.

"It looks good on you."

I turn to a wall mirror. The jacket is enormous, going almost to my knees. I cinch it in tight.

Mack comes up behind me, his chin on my shoulder. "You'd make a killer Mrs. Claus. What will it take to get you naked in that suit of mine?"

A hot thrill bolts through me. "Maybe you only have to ask."

A throaty growl escapes him. "Please, Mrs. Claus, make me the happiest Santa on earth."

I laugh. "Who might come down here?"

"It's never anyone but me and the occasional elf," he says. "And the elves have gone home." He pulls me close enough that his beard tickles my cheek. "Besides, when have you ever been afraid of a little risk?"

Gauntlet thrown.

I turn from the mirror and step away from him. "Hmm. So you're suggesting something here in the mall?" I reach inside the jacket and unzip my skirt. It falls to the ground as I walk, and I step out of it.

Mack sucks in a breath. "I am."

I start unbuttoning my silk blouse, hidden in the fur. "You promising me a good time?" I draw an arm inside the shirt to get out of the sleeve, then slip it back into the arm of the Santa jacket.

"Absolutely."

I slip out of the other arm, and the blouse falls in my wake.

"How can I be sure?" I'm glad for a front-hook bra today, pinching the snap through the jacket and slipping the straps over each shoulder. I wait for him to answer.

"Satisfaction guaranteed." Mack stands by the stairs, his arms crossed over the tight white undershirt. He's still in the hair and beard, so he looks very unlike himself. But he's right. He's not a postcard Santa with miles of white curls. It looks like something a distinguished older gentleman might grow.

And I like it.

I let the bra fall.

His eyebrows lift. I can see a shift in those velvety Santa pants. I hold the top of the jacket to me as I part the jacket just enough to find the lace of my panties.

"Damn, Rory," he says as my bare leg appears. I'm wearing my heels from work.

I let the panties fall, whipping the jacket closed.

I step out of them and observe the trail of clothes. "If someone comes down here…"

He moves for me like a jungle cat, and I dash to evade his grasp. I run to the other side of the bench, trying to keep the Santa jacket closed. "You'll have to catch me!"

His throaty laugh is like a rumble through my body. "You're on."

He comes for me, but I dash around the bench again. He leaps over it, narrowly missing the fur edge flying behind me.

I lunge for the stairs, tearing up them with little regard for what happens to the jacket as I go. I know we're concealed in the snow mountain. I'm giddy and so high on adrenaline that I could climb the damn thing. It's exhilarating. I feel painfully alive.

Mack stomps up the stairs after me in his heavy boots.

I reach the top and flatten myself against the inner wall of the snow mountain. Frosty no longer turns above us, and the lights are out. It's much dimmer than before.

The mall is closed.

Mack's head appears. I inch along the wall with a giggle.

"I'll catch you, Mrs. Claus," he says, and heads for me.

I take off again, making sure this time the jacket is secure. If there are elves on the set, or worse—that same security guard as before—I'll bolt back down.

But there's nothing. The concourse is dark, only dim security lights near the walls. The set is deeply in shadow, and I almost stumble as I come out onto the stage.

I muffle my laugh, catching myself on the side of the sofa and falling forward over the arm.

Mack reaches me, and his arms are instantly around my waist, drawing my back against his chest. "You are a naughty, naughty Mrs. Claus," he whispers against my ear. He snakes his hand around me and through the opening of the jacket. His warm fingers capture a breast.

I brace myself against the sofa, allowing his hand to explore me beneath the suit. I'm so hot, so wet. I've wanted this for days. And now we're here. I'm on fire.

His hand slips down my belly, and I widen my thighs. I'm so aroused that when his finger slides into me, I start to quiver around it immediately.

"Mmm," he says. "Not so fast." He withdraws, and I want to cry out in need.

"Please," I say. "Don't make me wait."

"Oh, I won't," he says. "Good thing there's nobody out here."

He whips me around and clasps the sides of the

jacket, jerking it wide and sliding it down my shoulders so it pins both of my arms behind me.

He bends me backward over the arm of the Santa chair, and I'm exposed to him, breasts high, my head falling back onto the cushion, my hips pressed against him. If Jess were at her camera, this would be one hell of a shot.

He leans over me, his mouth on my skin, biting, nipping, tasting my nipples, tongue trailing over every inch of both breasts.

I'm on fire, scarcely able to breathe, focused on where Mack touches me. His beard caresses my belly.

Then he reaches down, fingers plunging inside me, thumb on my clit. A sound escapes, and Mack presses his hand to my lips to silence me.

His fingers flutter inside my body, and I rock my hips against the arm of the sofa, my head pressed into the cushions. He's a shadow in the dark, a blur of white shirt and beard, a form providing heat and the intense touch sliding more deeply into me.

He withdraws a moment, and I'm in agony, but after only a short moment, his naked thighs press against mine. I bite against my cry as he enters me and draws my leg up on his shoulder.

I grasp the cushion of the sofa behind my head, reveling in each punishing thrust of his body into mine. I can't bear it. It's too much, too intense. I scarcely recognize him in the dark, only his beard and a glint in his eyes visible in the dark. But I know his touch, his body, the length of him inside me.

He's all I've known, but all I've wanted. We're here

again, in this space, taking risks, being wild. I'm naked on a Santa set in the middle of a mall, surrounded in fur, his body pounding into mine. I love it. It's me. The realest me. The one I can only ever be when I'm with him.

Tears squeeze from my eyes. I stare up and am surprised to see the night sky. There's a big open skylight above the concourse. The moon appears from the wispy clouds, like it's smiling down on us.

We're back.

But Mack isn't done with me. He wraps my legs around his waist and lifts me to meet him, chest to chest. I hang on to his shoulders as they ripple and shift, his arms moving me up and down on his cock.

He walks forward, dropping down to sit on the sofa and arranging my knees on either side of him. He presses his face between my breasts as he clutches me beneath the Santa jacket, driving me up and down on his body.

I feel high, like I've done some crazy drug, the moon beaming down, the velvety Santa sofa cushioning my knees. Mack is merciless, mouth on my nipple, tugging with his teeth, plunging time and time again into me.

The ache is sweet, and the tension builds in me again. He holds me against him, grinding in circles, so deep. My breathing speeds up, I'm lost again, and the orgasm begins, deep inside, reaching up through the center of my body.

He bites the soft flesh of a breast, and all the places where he's branding me with mouth and hands and cock connect until I'm crying out. The lightning bolts through me, too much—I can't keep quiet, and the wild sounds echo off the empty walls of the concourse.

Mack releases into me in a hot blast. We hold tight, letting our muscles contract against each other, bodies in sync. Our chests heave together, and his face moves into the nook of my neck and collarbone, his resting place. His favorite spot in the world, he used to say, curling into it when it was tired or stressed out.

We've barely caught our breath when Mack tenses against me. Something's happened.

"What?" I whisper in his ear.

"The guard," he whispers. "Be still."

He lifts the Santa jacket up on my shoulders and tucks it around me in case we're seen.

I spot the beam of the flashlight cross the concourse. Did he hear us? Will he investigate? I imagine getting caught naked in Mack's Santa suit. Our old friends will simply shrug, saying they always knew this could happen. But the other partners at my firm might not be amused. It's a salacious headline. It would go viral.

I drop my head on Mack's shoulder, waiting to see if we'll be caught.

"He's almost passed," Mack says against my ear.

I nod.

Then he relaxes. "He's gone. Let's give it a minute." He reaches down to slip off my shoes. "To be quieter as we go." He squeezes my instep, massaging my feet. "It'll be all right."

I slowly release my fear, letting Mack do his work. He always knew how to bring me down.

After a moment, Mack helps me silently slide off his

body to stand. We make our way carefully to the stairs and the green room.

"You're amazing," he says when we're safely down. "Worth every risk, a thousand times."

I let his words fall over me. I wish I was more care-free, that I could toss caution to the wind all the time and not feel so much regret after being impulsive. But some things about me do not change.

18

MACK

13 DAYS TO CHRISTMAS

I should be thrilled with how things are going.

Rory and I gave up waiting until the weekend. She's figured out exactly how much sleep is necessary, and we spend our evenings after my mall Santa work together. She's started taking naps when she gets home from work to avoid being too tired in the morning. She's what you might call a *strategic planner*.

I'm glad we figured that part out.

At the same time, something's missing.

The sex is good. Hell yes, it is.

And I'm always excited to see her. Definitely true.

But something about when she leaves doesn't feel quite right.

It's Monday morning, eleven days since Rory showed up at the mall the first time.

I've made some coffee and wait for her to come

downstairs to fetch it. We spend most nights at her place due to Sir Winston, but last night we stayed here.

I hear her singing, and it makes me smile. Rory does that. She has so much dimension to her. She's devoted to work, to getting things right, to rising to the top.

But then she's so chaotic, so wild, so incredibly free to be what she wants when we're together. It's a happy place for her. It always was. And Rory sings when she's happy.

My place is evidence of how we crash into each other. Cushions on the floor, pillows strewn all around. There are half-empty wine glasses on the coffee table. And it looks like there's a spill on the rug. It's fine.

I'm glad I have her back.

She's down to a light humming as she comes down the stairs. Her steps are slow and measured. She's already slipping into lawyer Rory, not the wildling I knew half the night.

She isn't dressed for work yet. She'll go home first and walk Sir Winston before preparing for her day. It's early. Earlier than I'd normally get up. Her jogging shoes appear first between the slats of the stair railing. Then black yoga pants. A fitted shirt. I try not to react to them. Our routine is set. She won't miss her first meeting of the day, not again. I have to keep myself under wraps after six a.m.

Her hair is twisted into a messy bun and her expression is relaxed when she sees me. I hand her the travel mug of coffee with one spoonful of creamer and a single cube of sugar.

She takes the mug and leans in for a farewell kiss. "See you later."

Her lips are warm and familiar. "Can't wait."

She glances over the wreck of a living room. "I should have picked that up."

"I'll get to it later." She seems concerned, so I say, "Do you know why Pavlov's hair was so messy?"

"You mean Pavlov like the scientist who did experiments?"

"That one."

"This is a dad joke, isn't it?"

"Maybe."

She sighs, but she's smiling. "So why is Pavlov's hair so messy?"

"Because he didn't condition it."

She shakes her head and leans in for one last kiss. "Your routine needs work."

"Five-year-olds laugh."

"Five-year-olds don't know who Pavlov is."

"They will now."

She shakes her head at me, then she's out the door. The ritual feels domestic, like a husband and wife.

But it's not.

She's not my wife. We've made no promises to each other.

So the nagging thought that's plagued me for days returns.

How will this end?

I doubt it will be soon. We had two years last time before circumstances drove us apart.

What will do us in this time? A job change? Another opportunity? Pressure from work that cuts into our time?

Do I want to wait for that? Should I quit her before it's too late?

She's not different, despite the intervening years. The only thing that's changed about Rory is where she lives and how she dresses. She knows what she wants, she gets it, and then she moves on to the next thing.

But me. I'm not the same.

For one, I know what it's like to live without Rory. This is making me hold on to this new time with her. But I also know what isn't there. Connection. Commitment.

These problems aren't going to resolve themselves, but I have no idea how to tackle them. Instead of sitting on my sofa, hunched over like a dying man, I should take a page from Rory's playbook and get on with my day.

I head to the shower. The chaos of my bedroom makes me smile—did we knock a lamp off the side table? I get dressed and review my calendar for the day. Two meetings and just enough time to get home and prep my Santa outfit before heading to the mall.

Then to Rory's place.

It's a cycle. And I'll be damned if I know how to break it.

19

RORY

Jerome buzzes me on the phone after lunch to let me know my next client is here. "Do you want to see them in your office or the conference room?"

"This is only a consultation, correct?"

Jerome's voice has a deep edge, the one he uses when there's someone he considers *tasty* in the waiting area. "That's what they say."

"Still no indication of what they want?"

"Just a business consult. They own a delicatessen chain."

"Okay, send them in here."

"I'm happy to come and take notes."

Hmm. They must be *very* tasty. "That's all right. I'll call for you if I need backup."

"Aye-aye."

I stand up from my chair as the door opens. Jerome leads three men into my office, barely able to keep his eyes in his head.

And he's right. The men are devastatingly handsome. All three are dressed casually for a business appointment, pressed pants and button-downs, no ties or jackets. These aren't CEO types.

One is dark-haired and charismatic, practically filling the room with his smile. The second one looks like he could bench-press my desk. His shoulders barely fit through the door.

The third one catches my eye with an expression of hope and excitement that makes me wonder what is going on.

I gesture to the sofa and chair. "Have a seat, gentlemen." I roll my chair closer. It will make me slightly taller, a power position I use when I feel outnumbered.

Jerome slips out, eyes on the men as long as possible. By the time I've arranged myself in the chair, the first two are on the sofa, the third, the more emotional one, in the armchair.

"I understand you own a chain of restaurants," I say. "I'm Rory Sheffield, and I specialize in business contracts, trademarks, mergers, and acquisitions."

"Rory," the one in the armchair says, as if it's a prayer or something.

I hold my smile in place. This is weird.

The tricked-out one speaks first. "I'm Max Pickle. This is my oldest brother Jason, and this is our baby brother Anthony."

Recognition registers. "Oh! You own the Pickle delis. I've been to the one here in L.A."

"That one's mine," Max says. "Jason owns one in Austin, Texas. Anthony opened one in Boulder, plus there's the original in Manhattan."

I relax a little. "So what can I help you with? Do you have a trademark dispute? Are you hoping to acquire another chain?"

Max glances at his brothers. "It's more of a personal matter."

My stomach falls. I immediately think of Mack. Does this have to do with him? Are these men somehow connected? I don't have many personal matters in my life.

"You have my attention," I say.

Jason speaks up. "The three of us recently got those genetics kits, you know the ones. You spit in a tube."

Anthony talks next. "You did one yourself. About a year ago."

How do they know this? My uncle got everyone a kit for Christmas. Mother took mine away, and the urgency with which she dropped it down the incinerator chute of her apartment building made me wonder what she was hiding.

So I bought my own.

It showed almost nothing. Just my uncle and grandparents, who all did their tests. Mom skipped. Nothing earth-shattering that would warrant her aggression about it.

I haven't logged in since.

"I assume you're here to say you are related to me." I hold my voice level.

The three men look at each other. It's Max who drops the bombshell.

"You're our sister."

I launch from my chair. "What are you talking about?"

Max also stands up. "Our grandmother got us kits as early Christmas gifts. She thought it would be fun this year to put up ornaments with every family member we could find. We have lots of cousins, more than we've kept track of."

Now Jason stands. "Our mother died a decade ago. We lost contact with parts of her side. People have been born and married. We wanted to find them all again, and the app lets you do that."

"But you found me, too."

Max nods, his eyes steady on mine. "We found you."

Nobody speaks for long minutes. Anthony is still in the chair, his chin in his fist. He looks agonized.

"Let me log in myself," I say, and return to my desk. I almost sit out of habit, but catch myself before I crash to the floor. My chair is on the other side of the room.

Max rolls it over, then returns to the sofa. They sit and wait, quiet and watchful.

I have forgotten my password, so I have to reset it via email. The process feels like it takes forever. Finally, I'm in. Sure enough, I have several notifications. I never allowed the app to email me, so they're all lined up unread.

New DNA match.
New DNA match.
New DNA match.
New message.
New message.
New message.

"We tried contacting you through the app, but you never responded," Anthony says.

"I told them to let it go," Max says, his voice a rumble.

"But I couldn't," Anthony says. "You're our *sister*."

There are too many links to click on, and I can't process everything in front of me. I turn back to the men. "I assume you've figured out the connection."

Anthony nods. "It's our dad."

I stand up. "Your dad was with my mom?"

Jason also stands. "No. They never met."

I sit down again. "You're not making any sense."

The three of them gather around my desk. Max elbows Jason. "You tell it."

Jason runs a hand through his short, dark hair. "This was a shock to us, too. We always thought I was the eldest. I mean, you may not even be the eldest before this is over."

A bolt of shock splinters through me again. "What did your dad do?"

"Jason, you're making a mess of this." Max turns to me. "Dad was a sperm donor, decades ago, back when his dad died and his mom was barely getting by. He sold it for money and made sure they didn't lose the first family deli."

Understanding thunders down to my belly. Mom always refused to say who my father was. I had no name on my birth certificate. She said he was inconsequential.

Never that he was a sperm donor.

"Did your dad take the test?" I ask.

"He didn't learn about Grammy Alma's gift until

we'd already sent ours off," Max says. "But he couldn't have stopped it. He fessed up immediately."

"Are there others?" I ask.

"Not so far," Jason says. "When we did it, only you turned up as a sibling. Dad doesn't want to put his in. He's not sure he's ready for a bunch of unexpected kids to find him."

"Do you think this has implications for your business?" I push any other thoughts away, ready to get back to legal things, black-and-white law.

The men glance at each other again. "I don't think so," Anthony says. "We have very solid contracts about the ownership of the chain."

"You might want me to check the language of that agreement," I say. "Make sure additional children don't try to sue for a percentage."

"Our lawyer is great," Jason says, but Max elbows him hard enough that he's knocked aside. "Hey!"

"We'd be glad for you to look it over," Max says. "Thank you for that."

"We're not here about legalities," Anthony says. "I have a sister." He clears this throat. "I always wanted a sister."

I feel like the Grinch. Here are these men, family, come to see me. But I can barely catch my breath. It's too much, all this information. And why did my mother lie?

"This is a lot," I manage to say. "I need to process all this."

"It's a lot for Dad, too," Anthony says. "He never

guessed when he donated all those years ago that he would ever know the kids that came out of it."

I draw a steadying breath. "Does he not want to know them?"

Another glance between them.

"We're working on that," Anthony says. "But we had to come meet you. I hope you don't mind. It's a big deal to us—to me."

He's the softie of the bunch.

"Can we take you to dinner?" Anthony asks. "Or we can schedule a business meeting. I can bring paperwork. Contracts. Whatever your fee is, it's fine. We'll pay it."

He really is anxious to know me.

"Leave your phone numbers," I say. "Let me figure some things out before we proceed. I need to talk to my mother."

"Of course," Max says. "We'll give our information to your assistant." He glances around the office. "This is a great place. We're pleased to see you've done so well."

I can only nod.

The three of them file out, Anthony looking back even as the door closes. When they're finally gone, I practically collapse on my desk.

What just happened? What in the world?

Jerome gives his signature knock, and I barely have time to compose myself before he's inside.

"So who were those hunkalicious men?"

I don't intend to blurt it out, but I do. "Those, apparently, are my brothers."

"You never told me you had a big family!" Jerome perches on my desk. "Will they be back?"

"Looks like it. And I have some reckoning to do with my mother."

"Uh oh. Was this a secret? Did somebody do some playing on the side?"

I ignore the question. "What else do I have today?" I ask him.

"Just delivering the Beringer report. Alaina can handle it. And, of course, the rescheduled patent meeting with Jacobson from last week."

I pick up my purse. "Get it handled."

"Where are you going?"

"I'm going to see my mother."

Jerome snaps the air, which is totally out of sync with his bespoke suit. "Go get you that drama."

I hurry to my car. The drama has already found me.

20

MACK

I'M SURPRISED TO SEE A MIDDAY TEXT FROM RORY. SHE'S strict about separating her work and personal life, and that extends to sexting.

Not that she's sexted me here. In fact, the tone is very un-Rory-like.

Are you available? I need you.

I'm supposed to have a second lunch with one of my soccer player clients, but it's just a check-in. I can cancel. *Absolutely. Where and when?*

Stringy's Steaks. You know it?

Of course I do. It's a legend. And way on the east side of L.A., almost out of town. *Yes. When?*

Now. I'm almost there.

I jump up from my desk and snatch up my keys. "Daisy?"

The receptionist turns from her computer monitor as I whip into the hall. "Yeah, Mack?"

"Call Ricardo and cancel. I have a personal matter."

"Everything okay?"

"Just a friend who needs help."

She swivels to her phone. "Should I reschedule?"

"Hold off."

"Will do."

I push out the door, texting, *On my way,* to Rory.

My worry is high, but so is my eagerness to get to her. This could be the breakthrough I've been waiting for. Rory is in distress, and she's calling on me.

It's progress.

I race down the highway, daring any cop to pull me over. I only start to chill when I've exited and pull into the parking lot of Stringy's.

The lot is mostly empty. It's well past the lunch hour. I only have three hours until my Santa shift, but I can always ask the morning Santa to cover for me until I get there. He's new and has been asking for more time in the chair.

I park next to Rory's SUV and head inside.

She sits in a booth in the corner, tapping on a laptop. She seems calm and put together in a pale blue suit, her hair carefully smoothed into a twist. I slow my steps as I approach. What's going on? I pictured gathering her tearful form against me. But she seems fine.

She spots me and waves me over.

I slide into the booth opposite her. "You okay?"

"Yes and no." She picks up the oversized plastic cup and drinks so fast that she takes in air at the bottom. A second soda is sitting at the ready. Rory is chain-drinking Diet Coke. I remember that habit. It's a sign of ultimate stress. There's also a half-eaten plate of onion rings.

This is a far cry from her perfectly balanced preplanned meals in matching containers.

I sit back and wait for her to talk. She scans her screen, clicks, and scans again. "I'll catch you up in a second."

The waiter stops by. I've already had lunch, so I just order a beer. It's five o'clock somewhere.

Rory's phone buzzes multiple times while we sit there, but I don't see the caller.

Finally, she closes her laptop.

"I have three siblings," she says, and before I can reply, she holds up a hand. "They're the Pickle brothers, the ones with the delis."

"What?" This is wild.

"Their father was a sperm donor in the eighties. Apparently my mother used the bank where he left his deposits."

Whoa. "There's probably more of you, then."

"Probably. There are guidelines now to limit vial distribution by the same donor, but back then, it was a free-for-all."

"Wow. I can't believe someone like the Pickles went around donating sperm."

"It seems he needed the money to save their deli in his youth." Rory picks up another onion ring and crams it in her mouth. "I'm stress-eating."

"I see that."

"It's going to go straight to my hips."

"We'll work it off."

She pauses halfway to eating another onion ring,

catching my gaze. "That will be good. When do you have to be Santa?"

"Three hours, but I can get it covered if I need to."

She swallows and takes a long drink of the second soda. "I won't ask you to do that." She checks her phone. "We have time."

"We do. Who keeps buzzing you?"

"My mother."

"Oh."

"I got her voicemail initially. Asked her why the hell she didn't tell me she got a stranger's sperm shoved in her."

"And?"

"She texted me back that it was none of my business. Like my paternity isn't my business!"

"What did you say?"

"I told her I was inviting every one of my fifty-plus siblings to Christmas!"

I almost choke. "Fifty?"

"It's a lie. I can lie. There's only me in the database. Other than the three regular brothers. So far, anyway." She picks up another onion ring.

"What did your mother say to that?"

Rory shrugs. "I'm not answering yet. Let her squirm."

My beer arrives, and I sit back and watch Rory. She's inhaling fried food and mainlining Diet Coke. The only time I saw her this worked up was when she was vying for the best jobs as we approached graduation.

"What's your plan, if you're not going to talk to her?" I ask.

"I'm waiting for her to come in person."

"Here?"

"Yup." Rory shoves another onion ring in her mouth.

"Where does she live?"

"Palm Springs. That's why I was driving this direction. But then I decided I needed reinforcements."

"So I'm going to meet her, finally."

Rory examines an onion ring as if inspecting it for flaws.

I wait. There will be no redirect. I'll get this bit out of her finally. We never met each other's families back in law school. She knew why on my end. I was bitter and never went home.

But I never knew why her mother was off-limits to me. She would stay with me for Thanksgiving, but was compelled to go to her mother's house and leave me behind at Christmas.

"Yes," she says finally. "I need someone on my team. Family has a way of pushing invisible buttons, and an outsider will have a clearer view."

Outsider. I shift in the booth, glad for the beer. "So is she coming?"

"I haven't told her where to go yet. I'm letting her get worked up. She'll feel pressure with Christmas only two weeks away. I've gone back every year, celebrated with Grandmom and PawPop, Uncle Thomas, and Aunt Barbara. She'll be worried I won't go, and that it will look bad to her parents and brother that I'm not there. She cares a lot about her reputation as a sterling mother."

"You'd boycott?"

Rory wipes her fingers on a paper napkin. "Maybe."

"Why do you think she didn't tell you?"

"No idea. I guess it's hard to admit. Maybe it was better to pretend she slept with some random guy than to confess to such a clinical thing. Probably she wanted to pick the pedigree of the guy. That I can totally believe."

"I guess they couldn't have predicted the rise of these DNA tests back in the eighties."

Rory sits back against the wood bench. "Nope. And now I have three brothers insisting I get to know them."

"Is that so bad?"

"I'm not very sentimental about family," she says. "You know that."

"I do."

"That was one thing we always had in common. You walked away from yours, and I barely saw mine."

Might be time to confess some things. My family. The Santa gig. I've held back, too. But before I can speak, her phone buzzes again. This time Rory picks it up.

"I'm at Stringy's Steaks in East L.A.," she says without waiting for her mother to talk. "If you want to come, I'll be here. It's about an hour from your office." She punches the *end call* icon with relish. "Thank you for waiting with me."

"Happy to."

She sips her Diet Coke and stares out the window to the parking lot.

I bolster myself for my confession. I've been full of

angst about when to tell Rory about the changes in my family, what's happened to me. Why I'm Santa now.

But is this the moment? She's really uptight.

She picks up my beer. "You probably have the right idea here." She takes a swig then grimaces. "Or not."

"You could get a shot of something for your Coke."

"That's an idea." She cranes her head for the waitress and, seeing no one, heads for the bar.

I formulate the words in my head. Maybe my situation will help her somehow. Feelings about family can change. Mine did.

She returns with an entire bottle of rum.

"I didn't know you could buy the whole thing."

"The bar was empty. I took it. They can charge me whatever the hell they want." She's in a pinch, after all. She pours a hefty amount in the cup. "I'll take a rideshare back if I need."

I nod. "Don't let me stop you."

"I'll probably want to bang you in the bathroom after drinking this."

I size up the cleanliness of the restaurant and make a passing guess at the state of the bathrooms. Not good. "You'll want some Lysol."

She plunks the bottle down. "Don't get practical on me now."

"You know I'm game."

"Good." She stirs her drink with the straw and takes a sip. Her eyebrows lift. "I should have done this before!"

She's going to be drunk. She can barely manage two

glasses of wine before she's three sheets to the wind. There are at least four shots in that cup.

I'm going to have to delay my Santa gig, no doubt about it. But Rory can't know. She's too practical to allow me to cancel my shift for her, and this situation is tenuous as it is.

"I'll check out the scene of our future crime," I say, sliding out of the booth.

"Good," she says. She's sipping hard on the Coke, turning the bottle of rum around to read the label like it's a Saturday morning cereal box.

Once I'm out of sight, I text the other Santa to say I will be late, but hopefully can show at some point.

I won't hear from him until his break, but that's fine. It will be enough time to make other arrangements if I need to.

I pop my head into the bathroom. There's a locking stall. I'm not sure if Rory is going to drag me there, but the way she's doing rum, it's certainly possible.

When I'm back beside her, she's on the phone.

"Mom, I'm serious. Good. Fine. Yes, I'll be here." She tosses the phone on the table.

"What's happening?"

"Mom was already in L.A. for some conference. She'll be here in ten minutes."

"Oh." I fiddle with a napkin. I guess confessions will have to wait. And bathroom sex.

"Come sit over here," she says. "I don't want her next to me."

She scoots down, and I join her on her side of the booth. She instantly leans against me.

This is good. "Did you look up your dad now that you know?"

Her head pops up from my shoulder. "I didn't even think of that."

"What were your brothers like?"

"Devastatingly handsome. One is clearly a jock of some sort." She opens her laptop again.

She types in *Pickle deli family*, and a host of images pop up. One seems to be some anniversary of the chain. She makes it larger.

There are three youngish men, late twenties. A tiny elderly woman with gray curls. I pause on her a moment. I swear I'm seeing an older version of Rory.

"Who's that?" I ask, but Rory moves my hand away.

"Look at him," she says. "He's an alpha if I've ever seen one."

The man is broad-shouldered, dark hair mixed with gray. He stands tall, chest out, and looks like he's ready to challenge you to a brawl.

"But look at the matriarch," I say, pointing to her.

Rory shrugs. "She's his mom."

"Your grandmother. Do you see the resemblance?"

Rory peers. "Not really. She's very petite."

"But the eyes. The expression. The toughness."

Rory keeps looking. "Nope. Nothing like me." The laptop slams again.

Huh. Rory's in denial. But I sling my arm around her as she returns to her doctored Diet Coke.

This is going to be an interesting afternoon.

21

RORY

When my mother walks into Stringy's Steakhouse, I'm glad Mack is here. She's seriously intimidating, even from across the room.

"It's Rory all over again," Mack says, and I'm not sure he meant to say it out loud.

I elbow him in the gut.

"Sorry," he says. "The resemblance is uncanny."

"She probably picked a sperm donor who looked like her so I would be her twin." I'm harboring many evil thoughts about this woman at the moment.

"She could've done that with someone she met, too," he says.

"Stop with the logic."

Mom stands in the doorway a moment. The hostess approaches her, but she looks around and spots us. She walks away from the woman without a word.

I hate that Mack says the resemblance is so strong. I would never walk away from someone like Mom just did. It's rude. I don't want anyone to think we're alike.

"Hello, Rory," she says. Her eyes rest on Mack. "You didn't say we were going to have company. I thought you weren't dating anyone."

"We're just fucking," I say. I know she'll hate me saying that.

Mack, to his credit, doesn't even flinch.

"Don't be coarse. I taught you better than that." Mom looks at the seat bench. "If I'd known this is where I was going, I would have worn my gardening clothes."

"Mom. You're the worst."

"So you keep saying."

She spots a roll of industrial paper towels, the kind you might find in a convenience store bathroom. It's what serves as napkins here. She picks it up and tears off a long strip to lay on the seat.

The cut of her suit is almost identical to mine, only a more solemn gray. I grit my teeth. I usually only see her in holiday outfits. I'm ready to burn my wardrobe. I can't believe we dress the same.

Mom's hair is cut in a smooth bob that curves to her chin. Mine is longer and outrageously curly. No blowout will make mine like hers for more than twenty seconds. This is something I must've gotten from my father, I realize. Uncle Thomas and my grandparents do not have curly hair.

Because my brain has gone this direction, I blurt out, "My brother Anthony has dark, curly hair too."

"Does he now?" Mom idly picks up a bottle of Stringy's fire-engine Cajun sauce, realizes it's sticky, and sets it down, rubbing her fingers together as if she's infected with something. "Are you going to at least introduce me to this person who is going to be privy to our conversation?"

"Mom, this is Mack McAllister. Mack, this is Pamela Sheffield. Who apparently can't own up to her actions despite the consequences to her child."

"Rory," Mom says.

"Mother." My tone matches hers.

Mack leans forward, extending a hand. "It's nice to meet you, Pamela," he says. "I've known Rory since law school."

Mom snaps her attention back to me. "You've been seeing this man for thirteen years and you never told me?"

I sigh. "No. We only recently reconnected."

Mom spies the rum bottle. "Have you been drinking?"

"Mom, you'd be driven to drink too if you discovered that your existence relied on sperm chosen from a list."

"It's not as if there was some other father in your life to be confused about," Mom says stiffly.

"You left me to fill in the blanks," I say. "Then you tried to destroy my ability to figure it out. As if I wasn't going to notice you trashing my Christmas DNA kit. Didn't you realize that was just going to make me want to do it more?"

"I thought my daughter would respect my wishes. You're not fifteen. You're thirty-seven."

"Right. Like age matters when someone who doesn't have a father receives the gift of a genetic test. From her uncle! He obviously didn't know either. Right?"

Her lips purse. "I told no one. And I assumed that if you wanted to know, you would've done it yourself by now. It is not as if those kits are new. I thought I was taking charge of an awkward situation on your behalf."

I settle back against the hard wood booth. "Well, it didn't matter. When I took the test, these brothers didn't show up. Nor did any others. It was only the family I knew."

"Then how did you find out?"

"My brothers showed up today. They wanted to meet me. They had also innocently done the test and found a random stranger sharing half of their DNA."

Mom stares out the window. "At the time, sperm banks seemed very discreet. There was no way to trace who had donated the sperm. I searched through a binder with information like hair and eye color. I got a few traits like athleticism and a sparse medical history."

"What made you choose this particular donor?" I ask.

"Same coloring. Intelligent. Healthy. Young. I don't know. I tried to avoid any traits that would make you look too different from me. That's all."

So I was right. "Why didn't you want me to know?"

"It's not something you tell a small child. Until you went to preschool, you didn't even understand the concept of fathers. When you came home with your first family tree, it was still too early to introduce the idea of artificial insemination. So I made him as unimportant as I could. Because truly, that's what he was. He was someone who sold his biology for money."

"Well, he's very successful now. He has a chain of

restaurants. Whatever he needed the money for, he used it well."

"Good for him." She smacks the table. "Good talk. I will see you at Christmas."

"Why do you think I'm going to Christmas with you?"

She fixes a beady glare on me. "Because that's your duty. It is the only time I ask something specific of you and expect you to do it."

"I expected you to be honest with me. Maybe preschool was too young, but remember when I got my driver's license? When I was asked why the father section was blank? Sixteen wasn't old enough to tell me then?"

Mom settles back onto the bench, her hands folded. "I can't help that some people are close-minded and made you feel uncomfortable, Rory. By then you knew that your father was never going to be in the picture. It wasn't a necessary conversation."

"Well, it's necessary now. You're asking me to join your family for Christmas, when I have a whole other side who is very interested in meeting me. Pitch me why I should spend it with you."

Mom looks aghast. "Because I raised you? Because I brought you up to be the person you are now? Successful. Driven. And you acquired a mate." She gestures at Mack. "Isn't that enough?"

A *mate*. Good grief. "I don't know," I say. "I'm questioning everything since those three men walked into my office."

"They shouldn't have. This whole DNA thing is rubbish. People should leave well enough alone."

"Well, Mom, I'm a lawyer. I can tell you that's no answer. There are affairs. Illegitimate children. Thousands of reasons why this matters. Your callousness in the face of my distress tells me all I need to know."

I think she's going to try to leave again, but she simply straightens her spine, her hands flat on the table. She looks to Mack. "Obviously you're close to Rory. What are your thoughts?"

I wasn't expecting this, but I'm doubly glad he's here.

Mack rolls the beer bottle between his hands like he did that first night at the Seafood Shack. "I think Rory is an adult woman with a strong mind and a truckload of opinions. You shouldn't bully her into the holiday break she wants just because it doesn't suit your idea of duty."

Mom holds his gaze, trying to bore a hole in him in a way I remember her trying on me during adolescence. She doesn't try it anymore, because I can win that staring match. The student became the master.

Mack is used to me doing this at him, so he's not the least bit intimidated. In fact, I suspect he's holding back a laugh.

But then, suddenly, I'm the one laughing. How absurd this whole thing is. I have brothers. I have a dad. A real, flesh-and-blood dad. There are probably cousins, uncles, aunts. My paternal grandmother has curly hair and looks a lot like me. I want to see her.

"Let's get out of here, Mack," I say. "You promised to burn these onion rings off my hips. Let's get to it."

Mom breaks her gaze and exhales a long, slow breath. I never talk like this around her. She probably didn't know I could.

For all I know, she's a damn virgin. She had this immaculate conception, and I never knew her to date anyone. Good for her if she wants to be independent all the way down. But I'm not her.

The wild emotions are making the rum go straight to my head. "Mack, I'm not up for driving my car."

He nods. "I'll drive your car. I'll get a ride back out here after my shift tonight."

"You're a good man, Mack." I lean in to kiss him, but my mouth lands somewhere near his ear.

He hugs me close. "You're an amazing woman, Rory."

He helps me slide off the bench, and the world whooshes beneath my feet when I stand. Dang. I'm drunk.

I hold on to Mack. How did I ever live without him? And why should I?

As Mack leads me out, I look back at Mom. She sits at the table, and the last thing I see as we head out the doors is her picking up the bottle of rum.

22

MACK

I don't know if Rory intended to go back to work today, but it's not going to happen.

She's wildly animated and chatty for the first fifteen minutes of the drive across L.A., and then she unexpectedly crashes. She folds over the console in the center of her SUV, her hair in disorder as it falls out of the twist.

This day isn't anything like I expected. Her mom is, though. She's a real piece of work, and it's no wonder that Rory has mixed reactions to things. Her childhood could not have been normal.

But then, neither was mine.

I decide to take her to my place. I need my Santa suit, and she can certainly drive herself home when she's sobered up.

She's all sleepy giggles as I help her into my living room and arrange her on the sofa. I leave her purse and keys easy to spot on the coffee table and cover her with a blanket.

When I set a cup of water and a bottle of pain

relievers next to her purse, I pause. Rory has a lightness about her when she's sleeping. She's relaxed, softly smiling.

I brush the tangle of curls off her forehead and press a kiss to her skin before I head out.

I ponder why she called me to meet her as I request a car to take me to the mall. Did she know she was going to get drunk? Did she need me as some power play against her mom?

None of it seems obvious.

Maybe it's too much to hope that she plain ol' needed me.

Mall traffic is ratcheted up, shoppers bustling from wall to wall on the concourse. I walk along the gate to approach Steve, tonight's elf handler. I wave him over. "I don't know if Ricardo told you I might be late. But I'm not."

"Good. Because Ricardo is so done. He's already told two little kids they're getting coal."

"Yikes."

Steve tugs on his tights. "Yikes is right. He'll be lucky if they don't can him when someone complains. And you know they will."

"They would do that this close to Christmas?" I ask. "The rest of us would have to take up the slack."

Steve turns to watch Ricardo wave a mother forward. "Go get suited up as fast as possible. We've got to get this man out of the chair."

It's a good thing I didn't need Ricardo to cover part of my shift after all. I hurry past the snow mountain.

I don't try to access the secret stairs from here. It

would be too obvious if a normal person carrying a suit bag disappeared into the set. Instead, I head to the employee hallway and snake along the labyrinth of corridors to the stairs that reach the lower level.

I can never see the green room the same way after Rory visited here last week. The bench where I chased her, the mirror where I challenged her to get naked beneath the suit, and the steep stairs where she raced out are all imprinted with visions of her.

I work swiftly, applying my beard, mustache, and hair, then suit up. I send Rory a quick text telling her I'll be in the chair, then secure my belongings in the locker.

I hope she'll stay at my place so I can see her once I make it back from fetching my car. But I won't hear from her until my break, and then only if she's up.

Rapid footsteps on the stairs make me turn. That's no Santa. The steps are too light.

It's Jess, the photo elf. She's upset. "Mack, we need you. There's a situation."

"Sure." I follow her up the stairs, under the snow mountain, and to the hidden entrance near the sofa.

The noise hits me way before I can see anything.

There's a loud murmur of a disgruntled crowd. A woman's shrill voice cuts through the roar. "You've ruined Christmas!"

Then Ricardo booms, "And you, my lady, are getting coal for the rest of your natural life!"

Oh, boy. I hesitate behind the hidden door. The kids can't see two Santas. That will wreck the magic. "You have to get him back here," I tell Jess. "We need a small gap so that there isn't an immediate recognition that we're different people."

"You're right," Jess says. "I wasn't thinking. You guys have different beards. You're taller."

"Go get him, then create a diversion. Make Steve do a dance party or something."

"Because Steve is such an entertainer," Jess says, her voice heavy with sarcasm. But she heads out to the set.

I can't see much, only the corner of the sofa and a bit of the line beyond. I wait in the shadows. In Santa School, we were told that sometimes Santas snap. We are human, after all, and we have limits. They suggest yoga and meditation and practicing calming breaths so that keeping control in tough situations will come naturally.

Ricardo is apparently past the point of no return.

Jess's voice rings out. She's on the microphone, which we use when we announce breaks or delays. "Santa's a little hangry," Jess calls, her voice reverberating in the concourse. "We're going to get him some quick milk and cookies and be right back."

"Don't bring him back!" the same shrill voice shrieks. The child howls with upset. They must be on the stage.

Jess doesn't address the shout, but goes on. "Our head elf Steve is going to lead everyone in a fun song. Hit it, Steve!"

I'm sure Steve's expression is murderous, but I don't get to see it. I hear his hesitant "Hey, everybody," before Ricardo suddenly brushes past me, aiming for the secret stairs. I grab his arm. "Hey, man. What's going on out there?"

He flings my arm away. "I got peed on too many times today. I can't have one more spoiled brat scream in my ear or kick my leg, or come anywhere near me."

"You'll be all right," I say. "This happens to everybody. Get out of the suit and go do what you gotta do until tomorrow."

He's already around the corner and heading downstairs.

A faint and rather unenthusiastic chorus of "Jingle Bells" filters to the back.

I wait until the end of the verse to put a bit of space between Ricardo's exit and my entrance. At the last minute, I get a brainstorm to pull out a candy cane and unwrap it.

I stick it in my mouth and rush out onto the stage, my arms in the air. "Ho, ho, ho!"

The singing dies out. I hold up the candy cane. "Candy canes are the best! I'm all good, everybody. That's a lesson to us all. Make sure you always have snacks."

I reach into my bag and grab a handful of candy canes. I can have Steve replenish it in a minute. I fling the candy out to the line. The kids cheer and scramble to grab some.

The parents looked relieved. They know I'm a different Santa. But I have to get them all back in the holiday spirit.

The angry mother stands by the camera, her arms crossed. She's going to be the key.

"Who do we have here?" I ask, getting down on a knee to address the young girl clutching her leg and screaming her head off.

The woman glares down at me. "This is Nancy. I think she's had quite enough Santa for one day."

"I understand," I say. "Some days I get enough of me, too."

Mom tilts her head. She has no retort for that.

Even on my knees, I'm pretty big compared to this little one. So I lie all the way down on my tummy, about two feet away from her.

The line quiets, watching and waiting.

"Hi, Nancy," I say. "You're bigger than me."

Nancy keeps crying. I rack my brain for all the things I was taught to do in these situations.

One trick is to engage a crying child by saying something clearly wrong. Their need to correct you will supersede any upset that they are feeling.

I start to sing. "Frosty the reindeer was a silly, goofy bear. He was made of bread, but the children said that his nose was made of hair!"

Nancy stops crying. "It's Frosty the *Snowman*," she says.

A laugh ripples through the line.

"Oh, right." I'm still on my belly. I pull another candy cane from my bag. "Frosty the Snowman was a candy cane, they say." I hold up the candy cane. "See, this is his arm."

Nancy smiles, then remembers that she hates me and frowns. "It is not. Frosty doesn't have a candy-cane arm."

"Let me try again." I pretend to think. "Frosty the Snowman was a smelly nincompoop!"

This gets her. She starts laughing, a good, deep one from the belly. "Santa, that's silly."

"Well, come here and tell me the real words. You can whisper them in my ear if you don't want to say them out loud."

She drops to the ground and crawls over to me. She whispers, "Frosty the Snowman was a jelly, happy sold."

I can't help but laugh. "Perfect. Will you help me sing it so we can teach it to everyone else?"

"Okay."

I have her. I sit up. When she stands, I hold out my hand. "Help Santa up?"

She grabs my glove with both hands and yanks.

I take a cue from the Three Stooges, overcompensating for her pull and rolling all the way over. Now the whole line is erupting in laughter. "You're strong!" I tell her.

She laughs and turns to her mom, who looks marginally less peeved.

Jess is snapping pictures. She'll know to give the woman free ones. I don't have to say a thing.

"One more time," I say to Nancy.

Nancy comes behind me and pushes on my back. I leap up and fly through the air, managing to land on my feet. "Are you Wonder Woman or something?"

Nancy throws her hands on her hips in a great Wonder Woman pose. "Maybe I am."

"Okay, Nancy the Wonder Woman, come over here

and let's sing 'Frosty the Snowman.'" I hold out my arms to see if she'll let me lift her, and she runs right to them. I put her all the way up on my shoulders. Steve is there to hand me the microphone.

"Okay, everybody! Nancy is going to teach us the words, and I want to hear everybody singing it as loud as they can!" I look up at Nancy. "You ready?"

One of the elves must've radioed the guy in charge of the music on the Santa set, because at that very moment, the opening chords to the traditional version of "Frosty the Snowman" begin.

Excellent.

I take a deep breath to help Nancy know when to start, and we start to sing.

If you had told me last Christmas that in a mere twelve months, I would be standing in Riverside Mall in South L.A., dressed as Santa, holding a kid on my shoulders, and leading a round of "Frosty the Snowman" in front of a crowd of strangers, I would have punched you in the jaw.

But I'm here. And I'm doing it. Even the passersby, arms filled with shopping bags, stress on their face, stop to listen. Some of them join in.

I've always avoided the movie *Elf*. It seemed ridiculous. People don't bust out in song to save Christmas.

But apparently they do. I made them. Maybe if a Grinch's heart can grow three sizes, one can spontaneously appear in my chest. Because if I didn't have one before I was Santa, I definitely feel it beating now.

So of course, my mind turns to Rory.

If I can change this much, if I can go from a man who refused to visit his family, who was motivated almost entirely by money, and hated to be around children, to *this*—then anybody can change.

I know what did it for me. I just have to figure out what will help Rory.

23

RORY

12 Days to Christmas

I call in sick the next day and have Jerome reschedule everything. It's easy to spend the day with Mack, since he's not the cause of my unprofessionalism. The blame for that lies squarely on my mother.

We laze about in the morning, starting with a sinfully decadent breakfast of stuffed French toast and a carafe of mimosas. Hair of the dog and all that.

And, of course, other activities.

Somewhere around eleven, I wake with a start, the sun streaming in too brightly for me to feel comfortable being asleep.

Mack is awake, tapping quietly on his laptop on the armchair in the corner, Sir Winston at his feet.

"You okay?" he asks.

"I feel like I should accomplish something today."

He reaches down to pet Sir Winston's head. "I'm game for whatever makes you feel better."

"You don't have any meetings today? This is the second day I've dragged you away from whatever might be important to you."

"You're important. But because of the Santa gig, I've given more responsibility to my junior agent. I can afford to kill a day or two, at least until I'm needed at the mall."

I tuck the sheet up against me. "I should start with a shower. I seem to be sober."

Mack grins. "Me too."

"I guess we could go somewhere for lunch. A good salad to counteract all that sugar we had for breakfast."

"Logical as always."

I pad to the shower. Mack seems to understand that I want to be alone with my thoughts for a moment, so he doesn't tag along this time.

I feel a thousand times better when I'm clean and dry.

When I come out, Sir Winston is still sitting at Mack's feet. "Looks like he's taken to you."

Mack glances down. "It's a good thing he isn't a tree."

I feel a dad joke coming on. "Why is that?"

"He doesn't have a lot of bark."

"Oh, Mack."

He rubs the dog's head. "I bet you'd get kicked out of a flea circus for stealing the show."

I sit on the end of the bed. "I know you're trying."

Mack closes his laptop and sets it on the floor by the chair. "Anything I can do? Besides bad jokes?"

This is the most emotional I've ever felt about Mack, so I try to gather my thoughts. "I'm grateful that we have horrifying family situations in common. I like to think that the world brought me back to you so we could spend this holiday together."

His jaw shifts, and his eyes skitter away from my gaze. Those are tells.

"What's wrong, Mack?"

"Give me a minute," he says. "This is big, and I have to get it right."

My belly flips. What's going on here? I know everything about Mack, past and present. Sure, neither of us had met the other's family until yesterday, but that was because of our shared disasters. I was always able to count on him to understand my distance from my mother.

Mack leans forward, bracing his elbows on his knees, hands clasped together. His expression is sober. "Rory, I would very much like to spend this Christmas with you. Nothing would make me happier."

I relax. This is part of the new Mack. Theatrics. But before I can chastise him for being dramatic, he goes on.

"But I will be spending the holiday in Alabama." Before that can completely sink in, he adds, "With my family."

Confusion blasts through me, hot and unsettling. "Why?"

He leaves the chair to close the distance between us. The mattress creaks as he sits down. He takes my hand in his. All of these gestures alarm me. He wants to get close, hold on to me. He's about to break something terrible.

"Remember that first night at the Ferris wheel? You asked me why I was Santa, and I said that I wanted to be *more*?"

"Of course. You were talking in riddles."

"I wasn't ready to explain it that night. You're the strongest person I know, and you came back to me in almost the exact same form that you left in. Successful. Driven. Focused."

"But?"

"I'm not the same. Early last December, almost exactly a year ago, my grandmother died." He's about to go on, but something stops him. I realize he's choked up.

"You mean the woman who refused to help you and Tanya with all those small children?"

He nods. "I resented the hell out of her. Tanya and I were the only teens. There were eight more kids, including a newborn, and Aurora wasn't walking yet. Our mom had just died from complications after having Betty Sue. That's when family steps in, right? But nobody did."

The hardening in my gut, preparing for a blow, starts to soften. "I know all that, Mack. Those facts haven't changed in twenty-five years. But despite all that, you decided to go to her funeral?"

"Tanya asked me to. She's never asked for anything since I took off for college."

"So you went back because you felt guilty for leaving?" I want to chastise him, but he's clearly not thinking straight. "You had your own life. You were under no obligation to raise all these children—ones your parents decided to have."

"I will always feel guilty for that, even though Betty Sue was already in kindergarten by then and the family could manage itself." He squeezes my hand. "What you say is logical, and it's what got me through undergrad and law school and working toward building my own agency. But then Tanya called."

"So what happened when you went to the funeral?"

"I found out that my father had banned his mother from our house. That his terrible relationship with his parents was the reason that his children had to fend for themselves."

I suck in a breath. "That's bad, Mack."

"It is. I blamed her for something that wasn't her doing. And then she died."

I stroke his hand with my thumb. "I know we never talked about this back in the day, but did you ever mourn your mom? I'm sure you were plunged into work with a newborn and all the children who needed basic things done."

"I didn't want to mourn her. I was pissed. I was only thirteen, but I knew that Luke and Aurora had almost killed her, and then she went off and got pregnant with Betty Sue anyway. I don't know why they kept at it when she started having so many problems. It was like she wanted it to happen or something."

There's so much more to this than I knew before. "Did you confront your dad at the funeral?"

"No. He wasn't there."

"He didn't go to his mother's funeral?"

"He was that bitter. The resentment went that deep."

"Oh, Mack."

"I was glad I went. Everyone's grown. Betty Sue is twenty-five. She's a pistol. Aurora couldn't afford to come. She's living with some ne'er-do-well in Mississippi. Tanya tried to send her some money to travel, but she wouldn't do it."

"And how was Tanya?"

"She was all right. She got married, and they have a little girl, Juliet. She's eight."

Something shifts in him when he says the name *Juliet*.

"Did you get to have a heart-to-heart with your sister?"

"Not really. Tanya and I were always practical. During those tough years, our only conversations were about who was going to run the baths and whether we had anything to feed the kids."

"So how did you find out about your dad banning his mom from helping?"

"Georgia told me. She's the next kid down from me. I was standing at the open casket, trying to see the woman I'd known in that gussied-up corpse, and Georgia walked right up beside me."

"How was she?"

"Impassive. She left right after graduation, like me. She's a high school teacher. She talks to Dad, though."

"And she told you?"

"Yeah. She said, 'If only our stupid dad had allowed her to help us, we could have had a chance at a decent childhood.'"

"And what did you say?"

"I asked her to clarify. And she told me that she'd only found out when Grandpa was in the hospital. She talked to Mamaw, and Mamaw expressed sadness that she hadn't tried harder to defy her son and help us."

Poor Mack. "So did you talk to your family then?"

"I was pissed, confused, mad. Mom didn't have any family to speak of, just a brother in jail, so Grandpa and Mamaw were all we had. After the service, I went and sat in the annex of the church. The ladies there put together some potluck thing for Mamaw. Grandpa was there, but he wasn't too aware of what was going on. He's had dementia a while. I hung out at a table by myself, looking over all the people. All those kids are grown now. All that trouble had moved on. We're adults."

"But is it in the past for you?"

He releases my hand and falls back on the bed, staring at the ceiling. "I realized I made a mistake. Two decades of feeling angry about something I'd been too young to understand."

And I thought my family had drama. Ours feels so clinical compared to death, shunning, kids fending for themselves.

"So why are you getting tangled up with them again? I thought you were all *to hell with it*. Was it this niece Juliet?"

He lets out a long stream of air. I lie down next to him.

After a moment, he continues. "So I'm sitting by myself. I feel way out of my depth. I don't even know these people anymore. They were all kids when I left."

I wait him out.

"And here comes Juliet over with a plate of food. She's wearing this pretty dress, her hair all long and curled. She held up the plate to me."

"You took it, right?"

"Yes. I set it down. She tilted her head at me and said, 'Aren't you going to eat? There might not be another chance if you skip.'"

Mack breaks out in a rough laugh and shakes his head. "This is what Tanya and I used to tell all the other kids. We were always stretching things thin, and if you missed a meal, there probably wouldn't be anything else that day."

"So she tells her child the same thing."

"Old habits die hard. It's how we know to parent."

"So what did you do when she said that?"

"I laughed. Like, so loud that everyone looked at me." His smile falters. "She didn't like that."

"What did she do?"

"She told me I wasn't nice."

"Uh oh."

"And I said it wasn't nice to tell someone they weren't nice."

"Uh oh."

"And she said Santa was gonna bring me coal in my stocking."

"Oh, no."

"So I told her Santa wasn't real."

"Oh, Mack."

"She started crying."

"Oh, no."

"I tried to backtrack, say I was being mean. But apparently eight is on the cusp of non-believing, and I put her over the edge."

I squeeze his shoulder. "What happened after that?"

"Tanya came over to soothe her and said I was upset about losing Mamaw." Another gust of air comes out. "And you know what that kid did?"

"Kick you in the shin?"

"Worse. She took out a prayer pebble from the pocket of her sweater and gave it to me. She said she got it from her other grandmother before she died, that she always carried it to help her think about the people she loved when she was sad. And it looked like I needed it more than she did."

I sit up enough that I can look down on his face. "Oh my God, Mack. What did you do?"

"I took it, of course. I couldn't not take it. She was so tearful and earnest."

"Do you still have it?"

"No, I gave it to Tanya to put in her stocking from Santa. With a note saying her grandmother wanted us both to have one."

"And you want to make it right."

"I'm trying to make it right. Not just for Juliet, but for all the kids who might have assholes like me telling them Santa isn't real."

He looks so tortured that I can't do anything but lay my head on his shoulder the way he likes. He folds his arms around me and pulls me more tightly against him.

"I've stalked all my siblings for gifts and conferred with Tanya about what they might need. None of them have much. I'm going to do it big. Even Aurora is coming back to Tuscaloosa for my party, I hear. We'll all be home."

I nod against his neck. "That makes sense."

He squeezes me. "I'd like you to be there."

My answer comes before I can stop it. "I need to think about it." It's my catchall for difficult emotional situations. I want to say something softer, but I end up repeating myself. "I'll think about it."

He kisses the top of my head. "Good."

24

MACK

Rory and I lie in her bed for a while, soaking up quiet time after all the revelations.

Her phone buzzes repeatedly on the nightstand, but she ignores it.

I sit up and snatch it from the table to pass to her.

"I'm sure I don't want to know what that is," she says.

"Want me to check?"

"It's probably work things." She takes it from me and glances at the screen. "Oh!"

"Work stuff? Or Mom?"

"The Pickles, actually. It's Jerome, my assistant. The Pickles are being pushy with him about having lunch with me today. The brothers who live in Colorado and Austin are leaving tonight. And they want to see me again."

"Are you going to do it?"

"I don't know."

"I think you should. Seems like you could use more family."

She frowns at the screen. "I've done fine with minimum family so far."

"Me too. But now I'm all in."

She seems reluctant to leave our safe position, but taps out a reply.

"What's the verdict?" I ask.

"You're a terrible influence."

"So you're going?"

"We're meeting at Max's deli. You're coming."

"Me?"

"You dragged me into this."

I twirl a lock of her hair around my finger. "This is fun. I don't know any of your family for twelve years, and now I get a mom and three brothers inside of twenty-four hours."

"Lucky you," she says.

It's already coming up on noon, so we drag ourselves off the bed, give Sir Winston a biscuit, and take off in my Maserati toward the east side of town.

L.A. Pickle is in an eclectic section of the city, some of it gentrifying, some of it still old-school East L.A. There's a gym not too far from the deli where some of the heavy hitters in mixed martial arts work out. It's made headlines a time or two in the past few years. I glance over at it as we pass by.

"You must go to a gym," Rory says. "Those biceps don't pump themselves."

"Yeah. There's one not far from my condo. I've been neglecting it since I reconnected with you, though. I might actually turn into a bowl full of jelly if I don't watch it."

She pokes my belly. "No chance of that."

We pull into the parking lot adjacent to the bright green and white awning for L.A. Pickle.

"How do you want me to play this?" I ask her. "Quiet support? Get the ball rolling? Divert any difficult conversations into football?"

"I think I can hold my own," Rory says. "But feel free to insert a random football statistic if the conversation dies."

"How about those Rams?"

"Exactly."

We've arrived toward the end of the lunch run. The tables are three-quarters full, but there isn't much of a line. The bell jingles as the door closes, and we look around.

In the far table near the back, two guys jump up and wave.

"That's two of them," Rory says. "Anthony is the shorter one. Jason is the oldest."

"Let's do it," I say, touching her back to move her forward through the tables.

Jason pulls out a chair. "Rory. So glad you came." He turns to me and holds out his hand for a shake. "I'm Jason Pickle."

"Mack McAllister," I say. "Friend of Rory."

The other one glares at me. "Boyfriend?"

Jason laughs. "Anthony, Rory is your big sister, so I don't think you can try to pull the protective older brother act."

I hold out a hand to Anthony. He shakes it, looking me up and down. It's amusing. Both of them are younger than us. But that makes sense. Old man Pickle wouldn't have been filling sperm jars once he was producing kids of his own.

Another man approaches the table. This one is seriously tricked out. I'm pretty built, but this guy could break me in half and still have a hand free for a sandwich.

"I'm Max Pickle," he says as we shake. "Rory, so glad you could come. Can I get you something to eat or drink?"

"We were going to go for salads earlier," Rory says.

"We have some fantastic salads here. Any vegetables you don't care for?"

"I'm not much on green peppers," Rory says.

All three of the men raise their eyebrows.

"Really?" Anthony asks. "Have you always felt that way?"

"Pretty much. Mom tried sneaking them on pizza when I was a kid, but I always picked them off. If they show up in a salad, I'll eat around them."

The three men exchange glances.

"Why is this so interesting?" Rory asks.

Jason says, "Because none of us like green bell peppers either. Mom used to go crazy with us picking them off our pizzas. She finally stopped cooking with them when it turned out to be all of us."

"Dad doesn't like them either," Anthony says. "You won't find them on our deli menu anywhere."

They're quiet a moment, as if considering all the ways they could be alike.

Max pulls out a chair for Rory. "Sit down. I'll fetch you a salad. What about you, bro?"

"I'll have what she's having," I say.

"Nah," Max says. "We gotta get you the Pickle special."

Now Jason and Anthony are grinning. "Definitely," Anthony says. "He should learn about the special."

"I sense a family hazing ritual ahead," I say. "Bring it on."

Max leaves again, and Rory and I settle into chairs.

The silence lengthens, and I'm about to insert the requested football commentary when Anthony says, "So we told Dad we met you."

"What did he say?" Rory asks.

"He said that whatever is important to us is important to him. And if we want you to meet him, then he'll do it."

"I see." Rory clenches her hands tightly in her lap. "I did speak to my mother about this yesterday."

"How did that go?" Jason asks.

"Not great, honestly. She felt it was none of my business that she had used donor sperm. She left it off my birth certificate, naturally. Mostly I didn't have any problems with that, other than a nosy person at the DMV."

"The father is blank on your birth certificate?" Anthony asks.

Rory nods. "That's how they do it with donor sperm. He's not technically a legal father."

Anthony stares down at the table, and we fall quiet again. This is tough stuff.

Max returns, dragging a chair from another table. "Food's coming."

"Rory told her mom," Anthony says.

Max turns to Rory. "You doing okay? Did that shake things up a bit?"

"My mother and I aren't exactly close," Rory says. "But she did not handle this well."

"You two going to be okay?"

"Sure," Rory says. "We're adults."

The silence lengthens again. This whole thing is terribly awkward.

I figure it's time to jump in. "So anyone watch the games last weekend?"

"Sure," Max says. "You into sports?"

"I better be," I say, "I'm a sports agent."

Max's heavy eyebrows rise. "Anybody I know?"

I list off a few of my most famous clients. Max and Jason respond with grunts of appreciation.

"Did you know Max is a bodybuilder?" Jason asks. "You think he would look good on a perfume commercial?"

Max throws him a glare that would crack glass, but Jason just laughs. "Maybe you're more of an Ivory soap guy."

"You're the one with the baby-soft skin, bro," Max says.

But I'm interested. "Do you do the circuit?"

Max shrugs. "I did pro at first, but I found doing the

natural circuit is more my speed. I wasn't willing to go the distance, if you know what I mean."

I do.

"He's got a fantastic ice skater on his roster," Rory says. "Gemma King. I'm organizing her fan club once the holidays are over."

"Now that's where Max ought to be," Jason says, dodging the balled-up napkin Max chucks at his head. "Throw some skates on that boy."

"You're full of it today, aren't you?" Max tugs another napkin from the silver box on the table.

I enjoy the easy camaraderie between the men, but Rory seems tense. I take her hand underneath the table.

"What are your plans for the holidays, Rory?" Anthony asks.

Rory goes stiff.

"We haven't settled on our plans," I say. "Rory might head to Alabama with me. I have nine brothers and sisters."

"Nine?" Max exclaims. "Do you have a table big enough for that brood?"

"We figure it out," I say, not confessing that I haven't spent the holidays with my family since we were kids.

"Well, we would love to have you in New York," Anthony says. "Grammy Alma makes the best Christmas dinner."

A young woman with a tray appears. "Vinaigrette salad," she says, and Rory gestures for her to place it down by her.

"Pickle special?" the server says, holding up a sandwich in a red basket.

"That one's for this guy," Max says, pointing to the spot in front of me.

"I'd fill your cup before you taste any of that," the woman says.

Jason shakes his head. "No spoilers."

The woman sets a pair of cups in front of us.

I pick them up. "Water, tea, soda?" I ask Rory.

"Diet Coke," she says. And there we are again. Back to the nerves.

While I fill them up, I watch the table from a distance. Jason is relaxed and jovial. Max looks like he's about to bust out of his green deli shirt with all those bulging muscles. Anthony seems overwhelmed. He constantly runs his hands through his hair, bracing his elbows on the table as if this is too much for him.

Rory sits ramrod straight in her chair, incredibly formal in her structured jacket and pressed pants when all the rest of them are in jeans.

She's feeling out of place, no doubt about it. I'm glad she brought me. Hopefully, I can bridge the gap.

I head back over with the drinks.

"And that's why you never want to be the first person downstairs on Christmas morning," Jason says.

I pass the Diet Coke to Rory. "I feel like I missed some important instructions."

"The boys tried to booby-trap Santa when they were kids," Rory says. "The tradition remains that there will be some prank to greet the first person downstairs each year."

"Why didn't we think of that?" I say. "Ten kids. You think someone would've thought to booby-trap Santa."

"So what happened the first year you did that?" Rory asks.

"Dad yelled so loud, you could hear it for six blocks," Jason says.

"So the Santa secret was out," Rory says.

Anthony shakes his head. "No. He read us *The Night Before Christmas* and reminded us that the father in the story is the one who throws up the sash and sees Santa Claus. He insists that's all he was doing when he got his foot caught in the snare we made. Santa is too wise for booby traps."

Max shifts in his chair. "It was so funny, we did it again next year. And we never talk about it, but somebody always makes sure it happens. Every year."

"I did it last year," Anthony says. "Nailed Jason trying to sneak downstairs to get into the Christmas cookies before anyone got up."

Jason reaches across the table to poke Anthony in the shoulder. "And the year before that, I set the trap and caught you trying to steal the last of Grammy's pecan pralines."

"Guilty as charged," Anthony says.

This is good. I can feel Rory relaxing now that they are regaling her with tales of Christmas past.

I consider the sandwich on my plate. I might as well get this over with.

I pick up one triangle and peer at the contents between two toasted pieces of wheat bread.

"Did you use the dill dough?" Anthony asks.

My hands freeze with the sandwich halfway to my mouth. "The what?"

Rory's about to snort-laugh, I can feel it. Her shoulders are shaking.

"It's the bread of the day," Anthony says. "Dill pickle dough. Dill dough."

I let out a breath. "Okay. I can't even tell you what I was imagining."

"We can picture it," Jason says.

Now Rory is really going, and the snort comes out. She claps her hand over her nose and mouth.

The boys look at each other again. "She's got Grammy's snort!" Anthony exclaims. His face has lit up. "No one else ever got the snort!"

Then suddenly, tears are in his eyes. "I've always worried about what would happen when Grammy wasn't around anymore. That we wouldn't get to hear the snort. But now there's Rory." His voice cracks.

Max claps him on the back. "All good," he says. "Now there's Rory."

We watch Anthony a moment, and Rory reaches down to squeeze my knee.

Instead of a football interjection, it looks like I'll have to lighten the mood with my humiliation.

"Here goes nothing," I say, and take a giant bite.

The heat sears my mouth like a flash fire. My eyes feel like they will bug out of my head. I manage to swallow the whole bite in one gulp and snatch my cup of water like a man in flames.

Because I am.

Only when I've downed half the cup can I come up for air. As soon as I set it down, the three brothers let out a whoop.

"You made it!" Max says. "Welcome to the Pickle clan."

Rory watches me with a half-smile.

"That's family," I say.

"Sure is," Jason agrees.

Rory squeezes my wrist. "Thanks for taking one for the team."

I lean over to kiss her, and the brothers whoop again.

I think they're my kind of guys.

And if I'm right for Rory, so are they.

25

RORY

11 Days to Christmas

When I walk into the office the next morning, Jerome stands up as I approach his desk.

"Rory, Mr. Heinrich and Mr. Blane are waiting in your office."

I slow my steps. "Why are they in my office waiting for me?" I check my watch. It's not even eight. Very few members of this office arrive prior to eight.

Jerome grimaces. "They didn't seem too happy."

I straighten my spine. "Did you get any indication of the source of their displeasure?"

His mouth twists in a funny way I rarely see on him.

"Well, spit it out."

"I know you don't have a lot of patience for Jacobson and his attempts at patents, but he's a very longstanding client. One that predates you."

"So he complained about how I was handling his

174

account to the other partners."

Jerome fiddles with a pen on his desk, and he is not a fiddler. "He might have been Mr. Heinrich's client before you came. At least, that's my understanding."

It's not unusual for the newest partner to obtain some legacy cases the other partners are tired of dealing with. It appears as though this particular one may have had some pull I didn't realize. "Thank you, Jerome. Please prepare all the documents for the Reynolds meeting at nine in case this one runs long. That way I can go straight to the meeting."

Jerome nods. "Absolutely." He sits back down. "Good luck."

I open the door. I'm not at all comfortable with the other partners sitting in my office without me present. But I flash them a modest smile and set my bag down behind my desk. "Gentlemen. How can I help you?"

"Come sit, Rory," Martin Heinrich says. He's an elderly gentleman and dresses very old-fashioned, always in a three-piece suit and cravat. He rarely takes cases with anyone under the age of fifty-five. And it makes sense. His mannerisms can be intimidating. But his power is undeniable. Some of the world's richest people run their legal work through him.

I move to the armchair, which the two men have left empty, sitting together on the sofa. Art Blane is younger, early fifties, in a typical office suit. He's usually jovial and easy-going, a good foil for Martin. But today his face is serious.

This is not good.

"Rory," Martin says, "when you arrived, we

provided you with a set of legacy clients to manage. It has come to my attention that one of our oldest and finest clients, Samuel Jacobson, has felt a bit neglected in his longstanding attempt to patent some of his work. Can you give me a rundown of what has occurred in, say, the last six months?"

Jerome nailed it.

"Of course. Mr. Jacobson comes in about every two months with revisions for us to review and submit if appropriate. Honestly, the last couple of rounds have not been significant enough changes to be worth going through the process. I have advised him of this, and we consulted with an expert in his field to give him additional guidance. We were supposed to have a meeting last week, but we had to reschedule."

Art sits back. My speech has pacified him. But Martin leans forward. "And what were the circumstances of canceling the last meetings, particularly since this would have followed up on alterations that you yourself guided the client to make, and which he was very eager to present?"

I'll never admit that I slept in after screwing Santa Claus half the night the first time, or that another cancelation was due to three sperm donor brothers. But I can improvise.

"I'll have to review my calendar. I do believe my punctuality and work record are particularly pristine. I am honestly quite surprised that you would take time from your day to quiz me."

Martin is not demonstrating any power plays. His demeanor is utterly calm. But generally you don't know he's angry until it's too late. I shouldn't poke the bear. But I will not be treated like a supermarket checker who's missed a couple of shifts. I'm a damn lawyer with a decade of experience and an impeccable four-year record at this firm.

"I'm quite sure your reasons for being absent lately are entirely critical to your personal needs and support your professional work," he says. "What I would appreciate is for you to provide some additional attention to one of our oldest clients so that he no longer feels he needs to call up the other partners to question the validity of our decision to bring you into our firm."

I seethe inwardly. This is not how partners are supposed to work. Junior partners, maybe. But my equity buy-in for this company was substantial, and I should be treated equally. Today, I see that I am not.

I set this bitterness aside and say, "Thank you for your concern. I will certainly prioritize Mr. Jacobson and will reach out to him personally today."

Martin slaps his knees. "Good. I would like to put this matter behind us. Art, shall we find some coffee in this joint before meeting with the Branson Corporation?"

He's throwing that name at me on purpose. Branson Corporation is the biggest corporate legal account in California. I've never been asked to do any of the work on it.

"Enjoy your coffee," I say. I head back to my desk.

When the two men have filed out, I sit very still and very tall in my chair. What is happening to me? In what universe would my fellow partners at my firm ever question my sterling reputation for handling our clients, and then shove their prowess in my face?

I feel small. Diminished. I've become less.

This will not stand.

I know it's Mack. It's obvious to anyone that he's led me astray. And now there are the Pickles. And my mother. It's an avalanche of personal problems. I've fought against this most of my life. I try to avoid complicating entanglements that get in the way of my career and aspirations.

Dammit. I smack my fist on the desk.

Jerome slips inside the room and closes the door. "That bad, boss?"

"I'm not in a good place right now."

He glides forward and sets a cup of coffee on my desk. "I can add a shot of whiskey if you need."

Right. Like I need more alcohol after the last two days' bacchanal. "I'm fine. Thank you."

"Did you guys settle everything?"

I don't look at him. "We did. Would you mind getting Mr. Jacobson on the line right away? I apparently need to correct some misconceptions that he may have about his level of priority in our firm."

"Gotcha. I'll make that happen." He points to the cup. "Drink some coffee. Take a moment. It'll be all right."

But as I sit upright in my chair, perfectly still, trying to get my usual calm to settle over my body so I can focus on my work, I'm not so sure. Everything is in disarray.

I need to get back to my status quo.

26

MACK

RORY'S CLEARLY HAD A BUSY DAY. SHE'S ONLY responded to one text since morning, and when I check my messages during my Santa break, there's nothing else.

This isn't terribly unusual. Rory likes to focus during work. But when my shift ends, and I still see nothing from her, concern trickles through me.

I text her before I start the process of removing my beard and hair.

Still nothing.

By the time I have completely cleaned up and changed into street clothes, I need to know what's going on. As I walk to my car, I put through a call to her.

Voicemail.

I decide to leave a message. "Rory, it's Mack. I'm worried so I'm coming over. I know it's late. I don't have to stay. I want to check in with you."

My concern for her nags at me the entire drive. Something's off. I wonder if her silence is due to her not knowing how to break it to me that she doesn't want to come to Alabama. Or if it has to do with her brothers or her mom. There's a lot going on. Maybe I should give her some space.

But I pull up to her house anyway.

It's quiet and mostly dark. There's a glow in the front window filtering through from the kitchen. She could be in there, making some tea.

I cut off the engine and text her that I'm outside.

No response.

Now I'm really worried. I picture all sorts of things. Rory collapsed on the floor. Maybe an intruder has gotten in and she's unconscious or worse.

My heart hammers. I walk up to the garage and peer in. Her car is there.

I make another call.

This time, she answers.

"Are you okay?" I ask.

"Of course I am. You're really here?"

"In front of your garage."

The door starts to lift. I kill the call and duck beneath it.

In the kitchen, Rory leans against the counter, a teacup in her hand. She wears dog-walking clothes, fitted yoga pants and a zip-up jacket. Maybe she went out without her phone. My anxiety settles.

Sir Winston must be tuckered out. He's sprawled on the tile and only lifts his head for a moment to glance at me before setting it down again.

"See?" Rory says. "All is well."

"You avoided me today."

Her lips pinch. "I try to focus on work during the day." Her hair is in a frizzy ponytail, making her look young and adorable. I'm desperate to kiss her.

But I can't do it. Something's off. "Did you hear from your mother today?"

She shakes her head. "No. She's assuming I will show up on Christmas Eve. And she is wrong."

I won't press her about Alabama. Not in her current state. I shove my hands in my pockets. "I was hoping to see you tonight."

She turns away, facing her electric kettle. "Can I make some tea for you? The water's already hot."

I'm not interested in playing any games. I want Rory to know exactly how I feel. I come up behind her and slide my hands around her waist.

"I wanted to be near you for a minute." I press my lips to the back of her jaw near her ear.

She says nothing to that, but I feel her resistance start to melt. It can be like this, and always was. When Rory got uptight over an upcoming exam or some assignment that wasn't going well, she worked herself into a miserable frenzy.

She would tell herself that I wasn't important, that she didn't need to see me. And I would have to worm my way back in, remind her that we're better together.

"Is there anything I can help with?" I ask.

She shakes her head.

My intention is to drink a cup of tea with her and go home.

But the road to hell is paved with good intentions. The taste of her skin gets to me. I brush my fingers along the nape of her neck, sliding the springy bits of hair away to get to more of her. The tension in her shoulders begins to soften.

She sets the teacup on the counter. A long breath escapes her.

I trail my fingers gently along the sensitive skin at the base of her neck and down her spine. I press my thumbs into the spots below her shoulder blades where she holds so much tension from being bent over a computer or a desk.

She groans, and I know this is what she needs. Attention.

I work my way down her back, pressing my thumbs along the indentions on either side of her spine.

She hangs on to the counter, letting the pressure do its magic, turning her rigid muscles into puddles of relaxation.

When I reach her waist, I squeeze both sides, making my way up beneath the jacket and a silky running shirt beneath.

Her skin is warm and pliant. I continue to press my thumb into her back muscles while massaging up her rib cage with my fingers.

Her bra seems to be built into the athletic shirt, and I slide my fingers beneath the elastic band.

She relaxes into me, bending forward so her breasts fall into my palms. I shift my hands up inside the support bra, continuing the gentle kneading, my thumbs passing across her taut nipples.

She sucks in a breath. She's mine now.

I press against her so that she can feel my erection

against her ass. Our bodies grind together, and I take my time, her breasts in my hands, my breath stirring the curls over her ears. Her hands are splayed on the marble counter in front of her.

My need for her rushes to my groin, as if all the blood in my body has concentrated in one spot. I release her breasts and slip my hands down and out of her shirt, reaching for the zipper of the jacket.

It rolls down with the gentle hiss. I peel it off her shoulders and along her arms to fall to the floor, then grasp the bottom edge of the shirt and lift, freeing it from her breasts and pulling it over her head.

I massage her more freely, revisiting all of the muscles in her back and shoulders and upper arms. She melts beneath my touch, leaning farther over the counter until her belly is pressed against the round edge of the countertop.

I fill one hand with a breast and slide the other down low, slipping it between her thighs on top of the slippery material of the yoga pants. I press into the seam, feeling the warmth of her and pushing my thumb against her nub.

Her body moves with me, but she quickly needs more. She kicks off one shoe then the other, knocking them out of our way.

I shift my hands to the waistband of the yoga pants, slipping them slowly over the curve of her hips, down the slope of her ass to her knees.

I lift a foot and step on the crotch, dragging them to the floor in one swift motion. She steps out of them, and now she stands in the bright light of her kitchen, her back to me, only a scrap of red lace on her body.

I reach around and tease her on the outside of the panties a little longer. She drops her forehead to the cool marble counter with a groan. I slip my finger in the panties and up inside her.

She sucks in a breath, grinding down on my hand. I add a second finger, curling upward to work her clit. She moans, moving her hips in a circle, pressing back against my jeans.

She likes it this way, but I know what works the best for her. I whirl her around, pushing the teacup out of our way, and lift her onto the counter.

Her naked breasts are at the level of my face, so I enjoy a quick feast, sliding my tongue along the heavy roundness and capturing the nipple between my teeth.

She arches to me, her knees on either side of my waist, her hands on my shoulders.

I grab the edge of her panties and tug them to her thighs, then take my time sliding them down her knees until they fall to the floor.

I pull back to look into her eyes. Their honey brown is stormy, her eyelids drooping with need. Her chest rises with every breath.

I cup both knees with my palms and, with no warning, jerk them wide.

She cries out, and in an instant, my mouth is on her, tongue flickering along the delicate bud.

I slide three fingers inside her, slipping my pinky along her body to circle the little pucker just reachable as she rocks her pelvis up.

She grasps the counter, shifting so I have full access to every part of her.

I work the heated flesh, licking her from end to end. I splay my hand across her belly, my thumb circling the nub.

She gulps in air, her body rocking, the muscles along her lower belly and inner thighs starting to quiver.

"Mack, yes," she whispers.

I love this moment, the trembling before her body unleashes.

"Oh my God!" she exclaims, and her body lurches against my mouth.

I press harder, deeper, working every finger faster.

The vibration becomes a pulse, more of her body involved. "Mack!" Her voice echoes off the countertops and the perfect cabinets and shining tile floor.

She moves against me, rocking back and forth, lost in the moment, as purely mine as she ever can be. She jerks, tightening, contracting, and gasps for air, a shuddering sound filling the empty space.

I do not let up until she settles, collapsing in, her legs falling across my shoulders.

I shift her to one side so that I can carry her cradled against my chest. She wraps her arms around my neck.

I pass the kitchen door to the hallway. It's a novelty, hot and invigorating, to carry a naked woman in my arms while I'm fully clothed.

We make it to her bedroom, and I lay her on the bed. I have so many more plans for tonight, but I have to know what's going on with her.

I sit beside her, caressing her body, laid out on the

comforter as if its beauty is made for me. I press my palms into the hollow of her throat and skim along her body, breasts, rib cage, across her belly, down her thighs. I work my way back up, keeping it gentle, waiting.

"Talk to me, Rory."

But she doesn't, reaching out for the buttons of my shirt.

"Let's get crazy," she says. "Do it again and again until we're annihilated."

She shifts around on the bed, reaching for the snap of my jeans. Then her mouth is on me, hands working the length. I forget why I hesitated, what I wanted to say.

The night will be long, and we will be together. I will get lost in her, and that's all that matters.

27

RORY

10 Days to Christmas

A notification about Mack on my lawyer networking site got me into this mess, and it looks like the same website might also get me out.

I stare at my screen, the knot in my belly loosening enough that I feel like I can breathe.

It's an update from one of my former colleagues at the enormous firm where I worked straight out of law school. My promotion there enabled me to buy into the partnership at this L.A. firm, but I'm no longer sure that I want to stay here.

And one of the founding partners from the New York branch is retiring. They'll want to replace him.

My job here is secure. I met with Samuel Jacobson, and we submitted his patents again. That all went fine. I'm sure the elderly gentleman had no intention of getting me in trouble when he took his concern to Martin Heinrich.

But ever since Martin and Art invaded my office to dress me down for the rescheduled appointments, I no longer feel connected to this place. Instead of a partner of equal value, I'm being watched like a bargain store stocker sneaking a round of Candy Crush between truck deliveries.

Then there's my mother. When I was in Boston, our lack of communication and visits made sense. A cross-country flight for the holidays seemed like a typical amount of face time, given the distance.

But when we live less than an hour apart, I worry there is something wrong with me that I don't want to spend time with her, or her me. I want away. Far away.

I send a quick message to my former coworker Inan asking if he's in the running for the partnership, since he's a junior partner. There are seven, and any of them could be invited.

Inan writes me back, saying none of them feel confident. The partners won't say it out loud, but the rumor is that they want a woman, and all the junior partners with sufficient experience are men. He asks if I'm interested. Everyone would rather see me there than an outsider, even if I would be in Manhattan instead of Boston.

I hesitate over the keys. Am I interested?

My mind drifts to Mack, but I set it right again. This is a career decision, not a personal one.

I reply to Inan, saying yes, I am interested. Within a

half-hour, Jerome patches a call through from Dirk Benton, a founding partner I worked with in Boston.

"Rory! What's this I hear about you inquiring about the partnership?"

This is going to be an important conversation. If Dirk tells them I'm in, I'll be up for the position.

"I am. I've missed my East Coast connections. I've drummed up a lot of new business over here, but there's nothing like a cool night that gets below, you know, seventy degrees."

He chuckles. "They didn't make you a Rams fan, did they?"

"Not on your life."

"You've been gone, what, four years?"

"Four last July."

"You keep your license up in New York?"

"I did. New York, Massachusetts, California."

"Excellent. That's a big plus, you being bicoastal. Let me run this by some people. Are you able to fly out here in the next week or two?"

This is perfect. If I go close to Christmas, then I can holiday there and avoid the whole debacle of my mother or the Alabama trip. I can already sense my priorities resetting. It feels good.

"Absolutely. Just say the word."

"Excellent. I'll be back in touch."

I set the phone down, my energy surging for the first time since that terrible meeting with Martin and Art. I am good at what I do. I can prioritize what's important.

I'm excited.

Jerome steps inside. "Here's the file for your two

o'clock. It's a big group, so you'll be in the conference room."

I stand up and straighten my suit. "Thank you, Jerome." As we walk down the hall, I ask him, "Have you ever wanted to live in Manhattan?"

"Hell yes," he says. "Everybody wants to do a stint in the Big Apple."

"If you had the opportunity to go, perhaps quite soon, would you take it, do you think?"

"In a heartbeat."

"But your relationships here…"

He grins. "Two of them are artists. They'll die to come with me on this." He narrows his eyes. "Is there something I should know?"

"Not yet," I tell him as we approach the glass wall of the conference room. "But trust me, you'll be the first to know." I take the folders from him and push open the door. This meeting is for a great contract I landed myself, and I'll be free to take with me to a new firm.

Heinrich and Blane can stuff it. Opportunity awaits.

28

MACK

9 DAYS TO CHRISTMAS

Rory gets even harder to pin down as the week wears on. After our kitchen episode that became an all-nighter, she is all the more elusive.

Even so, she's careful never to ignore me long enough that I come over unexpectedly. The behavior gives me a sense of déjà vu. She did something similar ten years ago when she made the decision to move to Boston and didn't tell me until she started packing.

I decide to make an appointment with her, using a made-up company name. I figure I'll make it to her office before she knows it's me.

Normally, I'm not someone who gets recognized outside of sports circles. Even though my clients often get spotted on the street, their agent is nobody important, at least not to the public.

So I'm surprised when the receptionist leads me to

a secondary office and an impeccably dressed man stands up to say, "Mack McAllister. Are you here to see Rory?"

He shouldn't know who I am.

I keep my expression straight. "I guess so."

He doesn't miss a beat. "She has an appointment, but she can squeeze in a conversation, since he's not here yet."

"Actually, I'm her appointment," I say. This might be too much to confess to an assistant. It will be obvious since he knows me that I came here under false pretenses.

The man's brow furrows. "That explains why I wasn't able to find the company to give Rory a briefing."

I rub the back of my neck. I'm busted. "I wanted to surprise her." I have no idea what he'll think of what I've done.

But he grins conspiratorially. "I'll be discreet when I let her know her eleven thirty is here."

I'm hoping the time frame of my appointment will blend into a lunch hour. And I will extol the benefits of breaking in her desk at work.

Jerome buzzes her office. "Your eleven thirty has arrived."

He rounds the desk and raps on the door before opening it.

I'm finally treated with the view of the space where Rory lives and breathes. It's a large office, her oversized desk set in the center. Behind her is a huge set of windows overlooking the city. She has a private bathroom and a sitting area with a sofa and armchair.

She swivels in her chair but, when she sees me, stands straight up. "Mack. What are you doing here?"

"I was trying to figure out a way to see you."

Jerome quickly exits and closes the door.

She adjusts her dove-gray suit as if nervous to see me. "You're my eleven thirty? Jerome said it was probably a startup, as he couldn't find anything on it."

"More like a made-up. I can throw a retainer your way if watchdogs are looking over your billable hours."

She shakes her head. "That's not necessary. I assumed you would be super busy with your Santa work during the week."

"Not until four. With the mall closing late, I go in later." I follow her every movement as she rounds the desk and leans her hip against it.

"I like your suit." She lifts my green silk tie. "I haven't seen you in one since graduation, and that one was a bit…"

"Cheap," I fill in. "But this one was a gift from the star quarterback from the 49ers."

"He has good taste." She lets go of the tie and leads us over to the sofa. "I assume this is a social visit?"

We sit down, knees touching. "I missed you. It seems your work life has kept you from even a quick response at lunch. Or when you're at home."

She drops her gaze to her hands, fiddling with the gemstone ring that perfectly matches her suit. "To be honest, I've been trying to contact all of my current clients personally and follow up on any loose ends that I've had in the last year or so. It's been quite an undertaking, requiring a lot of extra hours."

"Are you trying to get your numbers up?"

"Ideally, yes. It would be a good time for that. Closing out the year and all that, you know."

I don't know. I own my own company. But I assume that can be an issue in a firm.

The awkwardness between us is worse than our first date at the Ferris wheel. In fact, it feels a lot like those last few days before she left for Boston, after she told me not to follow her. We hadn't exactly split up then, but the end was near. The distance grew quickly.

Yes. It feels exactly like that.

"Has something changed, Rory? Ever since that day with your mom, you've been different."

"It was a lot," she says.

"Have you talked to your brothers again?"

She nods. "It looks like I'll be spending Christmas in New York."

My stomach falls. So she's made her decision about the holiday.

"Are you going to see your father?"

She manages a small smile. "I think so. He's willing."

No wonder she's been distant. That's a big deal. "Have you told your mother?"

"No. The last I heard from her, she asked if I wanted chocolate or pecan pie after Christmas dinner. I told her it didn't matter, because I wouldn't be there."

"Whoa. What did she say to that?" I feel calmer now that I know what Rory's been dealing with. I wish she had been going through it with me, but at least we're talking.

"I haven't heard from her since I said it. I'm not sure I will. I did text Grandmom and PawPop to let them know I would be stopping by a few days after the holiday."

"Can we plan a New Year's together, then?" I ask. "I'll be back from Alabama."

Her eyes shift to the side. "Certainly."

Uh oh. Her expression and her words don't match. Another wave of déjà vu hits me. "How long are you going to stay in New York? Is there a question about when you're coming back?"

"I'm not totally sure on the date."

"Didn't you buy a return ticket?"

Her smile is fleeting again. She can't hold it. "Of course."

But she still doesn't tell me the date.

A heaviness settles in my gut. "Is there something else going on?"

"I think spending the holiday with people I barely know is enough already. I'm trying to keep my options open on how that will go."

What she says is logical, but it feels off. Something's wrong here. She sits primly on the edge of the sofa, her knees tightly together, ankles crossed. No parts of our bodies are touching.

I can't believe that five minutes ago I was thinking about sex on her work desk. Because the Rory I'm seeing now acts almost as if she doesn't even know me.

But I plunge on. I don't know what else to do. "I chose this time slot in hopes that we could have some lunch together. Are you free for that?"

She nods. "I was going to do some phone calls during lunch, but if you don't mind waiting a minute or two while I knock a couple off my list, I'll be happy to go to lunch with you afterward."

She's so polite. It's almost as if she's talking to a coworker or a client. Not someone who bent her over a cliff and fucked her senseless. But here we are.

I can only say, "I'd be happy to do that."

As I fiddle with my phone while she makes her calls, alarm bells jangle in my brain. Something's happening between us. She doesn't want to tell me about it. But like her holiday in New York, she wants to keep her options open.

I feel like the only choice I have is the same one as ten years ago—play out this hand until all the cards are dealt.

29

RORY

I HAVE TO TELL MACK. I HAVE TO.

I've hesitated because I don't know what will happen when I go to New York. They may not offer me the partnership. I may still be stuck at my current law firm. I'll stay in Los Angeles and nothing will change. I see no reason to cause a big emotional upheaval over something that's only a possibility.

That's logical, right? Wouldn't any sane person agree?

But after Mack's appointment to see me, I realize I have distanced myself to the extent that it's impacting him emotionally. Sometimes I forget he's a Santa now, a man who almost ruined Christmas for his niece and feels he has to prove to the world that he has holiday joy.

I wish I could be more like him. But the next best thing is to be near him. If I can't feel the way he does, I can at least learn from him.

So as the extended mall hours come to a close on

Friday night, I drive myself over to Riverside Mall to make amends.

I'm not looking for a repeat of our insane night on the Santa set where we almost got caught by security. But I do want to show him that I am present for him.

And I will tell him about my trip to New York. All of it. He's a grown man. He can see as well as I can that this opportunity is merely a possibility, not a fact.

The mall is open late now that we're only a week out on Christmas. I arrive about ten minutes before the line will shut down.

Even at this late hour, moms wait with small children, their heads drooping. A couple of little ones are crashed out in their strollers.

Rather than watching from the second floor, I head to the gate. All the elves know me. Jess, the photo elf, gives me a quick wave. The elf at the cash register also nods in recognition.

I lean on the candy-cane border that fences off the set near the cashier. It's much quieter over here than the side with the line. Mack spots me and waves his white-gloved hand. He's happy to see me. He always is.

A young couple approaches with a very tiny baby.

"Who's this?" Mack asks.

"Natasha," the young woman says. "Nay-Nay for short. She's four days old. We brought her late so there wouldn't be a crowd."

Mack's eyebrows lift. "You must've just gotten out of the hospital."

The woman nods, pressing a hand to her belly. "Yesterday. We're leaving town tomorrow to see family, so this is our only chance to get a picture with Santa."

Mack smiles at the tiny bundle in her arms. "I'm honored you brought her to me."

Even I get a lump in my throat at that.

Mack holds out his arms, and despite the bushy hair and round glasses, I can see the tenderness in his eyes. "I don't think I've ever held one so little." The mother places the tiny baby in the crook of his elbow. Mack can't stop staring. "She's light as a feather."

The man squeezes his wife's arm. "We were hoping we could get a picture with you two."

"Absolutely. Come on up here." Mack shifts to one side of the sofa.

Elf Jess walks up to adjust the baby so she can be seen more clearly. The dad sits on the arm of the sofa, and the mom squeezes in beside Mack.

Jess takes her time with this pose, arranging the fur of Mack's jacket and the woman's skirt. "What a beautiful family picture."

"It's our first one," the woman says.

A hush falls over the concourse, and the music from the hidden speakers behind the set becomes audible to those of us outside the gate. It's "Silent Night," and the bustle of the mall comes to a pause as people take in the scene on the Santa set.

I'm not immune to what is happening. A family's first Christmas. A new baby so tiny as to be a rare and beautiful sight. A lump forms in my throat.

It takes a lot to make me feel emotion. I know this. I've always known it. I grew up fending for myself.

Crying meant a lecture about being strong. Waking from a nightmare only got me a warning to think logically about the actual probability of monsters in the closet.

There is no picture in existence of my mom looking at me the way this mother is looking at her baby. Or even how Mack is. There are snapshots, of course, taken by Grandmom or PawPop. My favorite is one on their front porch. PawPop took it, and right before he snapped, he yelled, "Olly olly oxen free!"

Mom smiled just long enough for him to get the shot. It only worked that one time. If he tried it on subsequent pictures, he got an annoyed look from her in the photo, so he stopped.

I asked him once why it had worked. He said it was what he used to say when they played hide and seek in the house. It meant it was safe to come out.

I always tried to imagine Mom playing hide and seek with her parents and brother in their rambling old house in San Bernardino, but I can't see it. When I was sixteen, shortly after the incident at the DMV with my driver's license and the blank line for my father, I asked Uncle Thomas if Mom had always been that way.

He said, "No," but wouldn't elaborate. I tried talking to Grandmom and PawPop about it a time or two. They played it off as a personality trait.

So if there was ever a lighthearted person in my mother's skin, I certainly didn't know it.

After the pictures are done, the family comes to the cashier to take a look and buy their choices. There are only two groups left to visit Mack.

I watch the couple peer at the screen. The baby

wakes, and her cry is so tiny, so light, that my chest tightens.

My mom wanted this. Wanted me. I've never asked her straight out what led her to have a baby on her own. Of course, until last week, I didn't know it was completely her choice. I assumed some affair went sideways, or a one-night stand had consequences.

But now I see it for what it is. Mom deliberately chose to get pregnant with me. She probably had to save money for it, find a doctor and a donor clinic. She might have realized she'd be judged by her coworkers and even her parents for carrying a child alone.

But she did it. To get me.

The smiling family gets their download link and moves on. The next family has finished up and heads to the cashier. Mack greets the last group, his smile as big as always, no weariness anywhere in his expression or tone.

He's a wonder. His resolve to right the tiniest wrong is something to behold.

I watch him talk to a toddler who can barely hold her head up. She lays her head on his chest midsentence and falls asleep. Mack looks at Jess and holds a finger to his lips so the image will look as if he's shushing everyone to let the little one sleep.

He always knows how to make magic, no matter what situation arrives in his lap.

He'll handle mine with grace and understanding, too. Even if it means letting me go a second time. That's just who he is, now more than ever.

30

MACK

I LIKE THAT RORY IS HERE. WHEN ALL THE FAMILIES have cleared from the set, I lead her to the back and down the secret stairs. Having her here has become familiar, like this is where she ought to be.

She helps me with the spirit gum remover, and we put away the various parts of my suit together.

"I have Sir Winston all set for the night," she says. "We can spend the night at your place."

"I like the sound of that."

We hold hands as we walk out to our cars. She didn't have to come here. She could have met me at home. But she's making a gesture. I breathe in the night air, feeling content.

"Should I pick something up on the way?" I ask.

"As long as you have a bottle of wine, that's all I need." She smirks. "From a store, anyway."

My heart practically sings on the drive to my place. I'm so glad I went to see her at lunch today. Now we have the whole weekend to be together, and I don't have to question whether or not it will happen. She's already here.

Maybe she's finally coming around after the unexpected news of her family. I should have known it would impact her like this. Rory prides herself on anticipating challenges and being prepared to meet them. Shocks like the one she got this week are hard for her.

After my shower, we curl up on the sofa with glasses of wine. She stares at the ceiling. "Did we get nights these like this back in law school?" she asks.

"Nights like what?"

"Completely chill. As if everything's going right."

So she's feeling it too. "Sure, during the breaks. When things weren't quite as stressful." I slide my hand up her thigh. She's back in yoga pants, the fabric cool and silky. The anticipation of being with her is intense. There's an emotional component tonight. It's going to be perfect.

"Mmm."

My hand continues up her body, skimming over the formfitting outfit. I bend down to kiss her neck and work up her jaw. Her shoulders relax and a long sigh escapes her. I kiss my way to her cheek, then down to her mouth.

She settles closer, and I shift us so that she lies beneath me. Each touch, every sigh, is magnified. I'm falling for her again. I've been ignoring it for a while now, but the feeling floods me as I make my way down her body, unzipping the top. She's not wearing a bra beneath it, and the thought that she came to the mall without wearing one sends my dick into overdrive.

I'm crazed for her and peel down the yoga pants. Her panties are the tiniest thing ever, a scrap of black lace strung together with two narrow lines of elastic. I flip her over, admiring how the thin strings disappear into her ass.

I make it a goal to lick every part of her and begin down the center of her back, reaching beneath her to hold on to those luscious breasts.

She's propped on her elbows, her chin turned to look back at me. It's so hot, I swear I'm going to explode on her.

I lift my head a moment to say, "Rory."

Her smile lights up my chest. "Mack Squared, back where you belong."

I keep working my way across her skin as I slip my fingers inside her. She drops her head, pushing back against me, her thighs starting to tremble.

This is where we belong, melting together, feasting on each other. I nip her shoulder, and she laughs. "Give it to me hard," she says.

I don't have to be asked twice.

I thrust inside her with such urgency that she gasps, bracing herself against the arm of the sofa.

Everything I feel about her is a tsunami, crashing from me into her. The past. The present. The future I'm counting on. I don't think I can live without her again.

I reach down for the nub that makes her crazy. We move together, the cushions compressed with our weight, the sofa itself occasionally shifting beneath us with a squeak on the hardwood floor.

I'd rather this moment never end, but when Rory

drops her head to her arms with an elongated "Oh" and her thighs begin to quiver, there's no stopping my reaction. Her contractions around me feed the release. I'm deep inside her, filling her, branding her as mine.

We breathe together for long moments, bringing it down. I withdraw from her and roll her back over so I can see her face.

"Come here," she says, drawing me down beside her. She slings a leg over mine, and we hold each other tightly, skin to skin, her face tucked into the space between my shoulder and neck.

The quiet settles. A clock ticks in the kitchen. A car swooshes by outside.

Rory trails a finger down my back. "That baby you held at the end was so tiny."

Interesting. She thinks of babies after sex with me. Hope flares in my gut. "She weighed almost nothing."

"It got me thinking about my mom's decision to have me. It must have been a lot, deciding to inseminate."

"How old was she then?"

"Late thirties. Maybe she felt her clock ticking."

"And maybe no relationships on the horizon."

"If she's ever had one, she kept it hidden from me."

Her hand keeps its steady slide up and down my back. This is too perfect. Better than when we were young. We understand each other.

"Mack?"

"Yeah?"

"When I talked to you this morning about New York and Christmas, I didn't tell you everything."

I resist tensing up. This is not where I expected this conversation to go. "You're not going to see your brothers?"

"I am. But that wasn't the reason I decided to go to Manhattan for Christmas."

"Oh?" I don't even know how to feel about the statement. I can only wait while she gathers her thoughts.

"A few days ago, the other partners of my firm confronted me about missing a few appointments. I found that highly irregular, and I was pretty offended. It's not like I'm a low-end law hack. I generate plenty of work for the company. I hold my own."

"I'm sure you do."

"I talked it over with Jerome, and we realized there had been a pattern of this behavior. Almost as if they were being condescending about my position. I didn't like it."

I'm starting to understand. "You're thinking of leaving."

"I am. I could strike out on my own. I could probably drum up enough work."

"Is that why you were calling all your contacts?"

"No, but it could work toward that if I need it to." She hesitates.

I shift on the sofa and sit up. I feel the need to face what she's about to tell me head-on.

She sits up as well, dragging a pillow to her lap as if it's a shield. "One of the partners retired from my old firm. It's not in the Boston branch, but the Manhattan one. I put in inquiries, and they asked if I could come up before the holiday to meet with the partners."

My stomach turns as I start to follow what she means.

She holds out a hand as if to stave off my upset. "I've been working hard to put together an impressive portfolio of clients to bring with me. The buy-in is tremendous, and even when I sell out my share of my current firm, I will need to take a substantial loan to make this move. But it would probably be the place I settle on for the rest of my career."

My urge is to let out a long gust of air, but I hold it in, keeping my expression neutral. "How likely do you think this is?"

"I'm not sure. There may be a lot of people in the running. That's why I didn't talk about it earlier today. Then I realized I probably should. That even if it's only a mild possibility, you should know I'm considering it."

So Rory Sheffield is planning to leave me one more time. I want to be positive for her. Excited for the possibilities.

But I can't. I was fool enough to fall for this—again.

"Mack," she says, "Professor Knoff would've taken you to the carpet over your lack of poker face right now. Opposing counsel could read you like a book."

I know she's trying to lighten the mood, but I can't help but say, "Is that what we are? Opposing counsel?"

"No! Mack, I'm sorry. I can look at firms here in California, too."

"No. It sounds like your mind is already made up."

"But it's not. It's not at all! I'm exploring my options."

"Right. The options that get you the hell out of here."

"Mack. This isn't about you."

"Of course not. It wasn't about me ten years ago either. I don't factor into any of your decisions, not the smallest amount."

Outwardly, I'm pushing anger at her. But inwardly, I'm already grieving. It's law school graduation all over again. Me putting out all the emotional energy. Her making decisions as if this component of her life doesn't even exist.

I pick up my wine glass and take it to the kitchen. "I'm going to wash this out."

"Mack!"

Moving to another room doesn't put much distance between us. It's an open floor plan. So I can see her sitting on my sofa, her back rigid. Tough-as-nails Rory. I knew what I was getting into. I knew what could happen.

I have to accept that the moment is here. This second chance we were given amounts to nothing.

Of course the old firm will want Rory. She's amazing. Brilliant. Driven. They'd be stupid not to take her on.

I brace my arms on the sink. She's as good as gone.

And this time, I won't be foolish enough to even ask if I can follow her.

31

RORY

2 Days to Christmas

New York is always a wonder. I visited many times during my years in Boston. I could easily take a train between cities and spend a weekend.

I did the trips alone, never managing to make friends tight enough to ask to accompany me on a train excursion. I always thought I would date someone amazing enough to escape for the weekend with, and that would be the moment we'd come together. But it never happened.

Now Mack won't talk to me. Since our fight, we've been out of communication. I went to his condo once, but he wasn't there. I even visited the Santa set, but Elf Jess said he was doing a hospital visit. A different Santa had his shift. And then I had to fly here.

I'm trying to feel peace. I'm surrounded with beauty. The Rockefeller Christmas tree is only a few yards from my bench. The air is crisp and the snow is gentle. I can do anything I want with my evening.

The meetings with the law firm went extremely well. I'm quite sure they are going to offer me the opportunity to buy in as a partner. If I do, that will seal my fate with Mack, not that there's a chance with him anymore even if I don't.

I'm headed to the Pickle home tomorrow morning, and I'm nervous about that. Something in the back of my mind pokes at me, saying this trip would be better if Mack were here. But I push it aside. I can't change what happened between us. I was honest with him, and it blew up in my face.

My happiness cannot be placed in the hands of anyone else. My mother taught me that. It was one of her most fervent lessons.

Of course, she's super mad at me, too. She thought I would show for Christmas despite what I told her. But tomorrow is Christmas Eve, and she finally texted me to say she got both pies, so my preference would be honored no matter which it was.

I told her I was in New York and not coming home until next week.

She called me after that. I was tempted not to answer. But then I realized the sounds of New York in the background would prove to her that I was clear across the country from her.

The conversation did not go well. She accused me of grandstanding. Then of forsaking her real family for this family I was never supposed to know.

I didn't say much, but listened as she vented. In the

end, I only told her I wasn't sure what made a real family anymore. That something about how I was wired was making it impossible to function and have a real relationship.

I might've said something about maybe the same thing happened to her, and that was why she had never had a love affair of her own. I lost my head for a while.

And she hung up.

Merry Christmas all around.

At least Sir Winston is happy. Jerome has him, and my pup is getting spoiled by all the loving people fussing over him.

My thoughts have wandered again. I want to focus on the loveliness of New York at Christmas, not my complicated life. The bustle around me is incredible. Everyone walking by my bench knows where they're going, and they are anxious to get there.

People carry packages, shopping bags, children. Some are serious. Others laugh. Occasionally a group of carolers will stand at the base of the tree and sing.

I wonder what I look like to them, a professionally dressed woman in a wool coat, sitting alone on a bench. But it's New York. I'm sure I go unnoticed.

I do have a few shopping bags myself, gifts I've picked up for Grandmom and PawPop. Then one other thing. The most extravagant item I've bought in years— a gorgeous Piaget watch.

I got it for Mack. I don't know why. I wanted to, I guess, even if it will always be mine and never his. It's beautiful, silver and gray. Something about it spoke to me about the time we've been together, the time apart.

I open the box and lift it to my ear, taking comfort in the gentle ticking sound.

I had it engraved, so I have no choice but to keep it. I don't know if I will get the opportunity to give it to him if he's not returning my phone calls. Maybe somewhere down the line.

His feelings are real and valid. I was untrustworthy. But even though his family situation was screwed up too, he did have the love of a mother for thirteen years, as well as a bond with siblings. I didn't get that.

The revelations of the last few weeks have shown me I haven't had many good family examples to live by. I should've spent more time with Grandmom and PawPop. They've been married fifty years and should have been a proper influence. I saw them too little.

Tick. Tick. Tick. It's a wonderful sound. It relaxes me, gets me out of these spinning thoughts. I should get back to the hotel. Tomorrow is a big, big day.

I will meet my father.

1 Day to Christmas

When the taxi drops me off at the row of brownstones, I don't know what to expect. It's the morning of Christmas Eve, and I've made this crazy decision to spend it with people I barely know. And yet they are just like me.

At least at the DNA level.

I head up the steep steps to the front door and press the buzzer.

Inside, I hear laughter, then footsteps approaching.

I bought a new dress for this. I didn't have much that was suitable. I couldn't wear a power suit. And I didn't want to wear jeans. The weather here is fifty degrees colder than Southern California, rendering most of my outfits completely useless.

It's a simple dress with long sleeves. The green material has a bit of shimmer and flows to just below my knees. I feel good in it. Relaxed.

I hope I'm ready for this.

The door flies open. It's Anthony. He smiles at me warmly. "Rory. Our sister." He envelops me in a hug. My throat tightens, and this surprises me. I didn't expect to feel emotional about this day.

As he leads me through a narrow hall that opens up into a living room, I know immediately this is going to be like no Christmas I've ever experienced.

The room is wall-to-wall people. Jason sits on the sofa holding hands with a woman with long, dark hair. Max is on the floor by an armchair where a very petite woman with her hair piled in a messy bun sits cross-legged in workout clothes.

I worry for a moment that I'm too dressed up, but then another woman enters from the door that appears to lead to the kitchen. She's wearing a flowing dress a lot like mine. I try to relax.

The second sofa is crammed with two women I don't know, a man, and a little boy about three years old.

The room goes quiet, everyone looking up expectantly.

Anthony turns to me. "I promise there will not be a quiz, but I'll take you through everyone's names."

I nod. "Feel free to test me. I am excellent with names."

The room erupts with whistles and cheers. It's boisterous and a touch overwhelming.

"All right," Anthony says. "Here goes." He points to the smaller sofa. "You know Jason. This is his wife Nova. They live in Austin."

"It's good to see you again, Jason," I say. "Hello, Nova."

"That's her trick," Nova says. "She's going to repeat all our names."

Another cheer rises.

I nod, but the real trick is to associate a word that describes the person and begins with the same first letter as the name. I assign no-nonsense to Nova, because she called me out right away.

Anthony goes on. "There's our brother Max. This is his brand-new wife Camryn. They got married last summer in France."

Camryn waves. "I'm sorry I didn't get to meet you at the deli the other day. I hope we can get together after the holidays."

"I'd like that," I say. I dub her Caring Camryn. No-nonsense Nova. Caring Camryn.

Anthony walks over to the woman who came through the door. "This beautiful lady is Magnolia. We are engaged."

"Anthony! You didn't mention that," I say. "Congratulations to you both."

"Hmm," Nova says. "She quit repeating names. Will she get them right?"

I simply smile at her. But I think Magnificent Magnolia because she is the most dressed-up of the group. No-nonsense Nova. Caring Camryn. Magnificent Magnolia.

Now we have the whole row of people I don't know.

Anthony turns to the long sofa. "Here we have the cousins. So my dad…" He hesitates. "*Our* dad has a brother, Martin. Martin and his wife Fran have two daughters, Sunny and Greta."

The two women on the sofa raise their hands. Oh boy. I'm trying to keep straight the people I have not met yet, Martin and Fran, who would be my aunt and uncle, and these two new women.

"Which one is which?" I ask.

"I'm Sunny," says a long-haired woman in a flowing print dress. She's very natural looking, with no makeup.

I will call her Straightforward Sunny.

"I'm Greta," says the other cousin, with a short blond bob. The wiggly toddler tries to escape from her lap, and she distracts him with a flashy spinning toy. Since she's clearly a great mom, I dub her Greta the Great.

"This is my husband Jude," Greta says.

The man nods at me, his light blue eyes quickly shifting back to his wife and child. Gentle Jude. Not quite perfect, but works in my head.

That's it for this room.

I quickly go around the room reminding myself of everyone's names and silently adding Martin and Fran as the invisible people I've learned about.

"Well, have at it," Nova says. "Show us what you got."

"Sure," I say. I turn back to Jason. "Jason is my half-brother, married to you, Nova. My other half-brother is Max, recently married to Camryn. Anthony here will soon marry Magnolia. On the other side of the family, Uncle Martin and Aunt Fran have two daughters, Sunny and Greta. Greta, your husband is Jude, and I don't think I got the name of this little guy."

Everyone claps for a moment. "Good show," Max says.

"This is Caden," Greta says. "The littlest Pickle."

"Actually, he's a Jones," Jude says.

"Every Pickle's a Pickle," Greta says in a low voice, as if she's mimicking somebody.

Everyone laughs, and I assume this is a longstanding joke.

Jason stands. "Are you ready to meet Dad?" he asks. "He and Grammy Alma are in the kitchen tending to the food."

Interesting that he hasn't come out. I wonder if he's nervous about this. His sons are forcing him to meet the product of his bid to make money thirty-eight years ago.

"I'm ready if he is."

Max also stands, but the rest of the family stays in their seats. I'm glad. Both for being ushered by the men, and for not having more bystanders than I can manage.

I've only taken a single step forward when Nova jumps up. "Goodness, boys, take her coat and things. Don't make her march in there like she's about to run back out."

Max and Anthony sheepishly help me out of my coat. Nova takes the purse. "Sherman can be a bit rough around the edges," she says quietly. "But he's pretty soft-hearted on the inside."

Rough around the edges. Okay. I'm warned.

"This way," Anthony says.

The kitchen is large and open, with an island in the center and a long counter running along the back with windows that face into a courtyard. The smells are amazing.

A tiny elderly woman with a mass of gray curls peers through the oven window.

"Grammy?" Anthony says.

She turns, and a huge smile brightens her face. "Here she is." She approaches, holding out her hands to grasp mine. Her eyes immediately fill with tears. "Not since the birth of Greta and Sunny have I seen a young woman as beautiful and perfect as you. You have my son's eyes." She glances up at my head. "And I'm so sorry for the terrible hair."

All my tension releases and I snort-laugh, and the three brothers burst out in chuckles.

"Sorry for that too," Grammy says, and lets out a snort-laugh of her own. And then she pulls me to her, her head grazing my chin.

"It's so nice to meet you, Grammy," I say.

She squeezes my middle. "We're pleased to have you

here for Christmas." She pulls away. "Sherman? Are you going to come meet your beautiful daughter?"

Sherman is still turned toward the window. As much as I'm glad to have this opportunity to meet these people, I'm not sure it's been the right decision for him.

My mom's shrill statement at the restaurant buzzes in my ear. *This whole DNA thing is rubbish. People should leave well enough alone.*

The seconds tick by.

"Sherman Packwood," Grammy says, and her tone is all business, as if Sherman is a four-year-old in the cookie jar. "I didn't raise you to be unwilling to face the path that life leads you down. This was the one you chose. And it has created something beautiful."

He lifts his head and seems to square his shoulders. He turns around, and the resemblance to his sons is remarkable, Jason in particular. His dark hair is speckled heavily with gray, but he is substantial, broad-shouldered and strong.

For the first time in my thirty-seven years, I think about what my own son might look like. Seeing the traits of these people passed down makes me realize that I could expand this genetic pool if I wanted. Not that I do. But this is what I would get.

"Hello, Rory," he finally says. "I'm Sherman."

"Thank you for having me in your home, Sherman," I say, confirming the name he has given me to use for him. He is, after all, a stranger. It's a long way from *Dad*.

"You're very lovely," he says. "And whip smart, I hear. You didn't get that from me. But I'm quite proud that you're a lawyer with a successful career."

"And I admire the success of your restaurants," I say. It feels very formal, but we are at least talking.

The brothers stand near the door. Anthony in particular looks like he is carrying strain as he watches this meeting go down. Grammy is near me, her arm looped through my elbow.

"Where are you staying?" Sherman asks.

"Midtown. I like being able to walk to Times Square. It's a magical place, particularly this time of year."

"I have to agree with you there. There's nothing like New York City at Christmastime."

Grammy seems pleased by our conversation, nodding along with a gentle smile. "So tell us about yourself, Rory," she says. "Have you always lived in California?" She releases me and moves to a center island where she's been chopping vegetables.

I lean my elbows on the counter. "I was born in Palm Springs, and that is where my mother still lives."

At the word *mother*, Sherman shifts back to the sink.

I ignore him and speak to Grammy. "I did my undergrad at the University of California, San Diego and worked a few years so that I could pay off some of my loans before applying to law school at the University of California, Berkeley."

"I hear that's a very good school," Grammy says. She doesn't even have to look as she rapidly chops the carrot into perfect razor-thin slices. She scoots them away, and the next one is done before I can even blink. She smiles as she catches me watching. "Seventy years of deli work will do that."

Sherman turns. "Boys, you should be chopping. Grammy is watching over the soufflés."

Grammy passes the knife to Jason. "Excellent point. Rory and I can watch the soufflés." We move back to the oven where we started. "Do you like to travel?" Grammy asks.

"I do, but I find it hard to get away. I'm a partner in my law firm, and that brings responsibilities I haven't quite managed to balance yet."

She smiles. "You're young. You'll figure it out. Work will consume you for many years, but then your priorities will start to shift. You'll find your way."

Her advice is so warm and comforting compared to the drill sergeant rules my mother hammered into me.

"What are you making in here, exactly?" I ask.

"It's a potato soufflé," Grammy says. "Everyone here goes bonkers for it. I have to make three of them to get through Christmas dinner without running out." She turns on the oven light and peers in the window. "I'm past the point where I can open the door anymore. Let's take a look."

I peer inside as well. Three French white Corning-ware ovals are filled with a lovely crust, slowly turning brown.

"Potato soufflés are not as fragile as dessert ones," she says. "You can barely breathe on those before they collapse."

"What makes soufflés so fragile?"

"The air beaten into the eggs. You want them to be light and fluffy, but as the air expands, it gets tricky. Do you like to cook?"

"I do it some. I meal-prep every weekend so I can bring my own lunches."

"I've heard about that," Grammy says. "Rows of perfect food. I'm impressed." We turn back to the kitchen island, and Grammy throws up her hands. "Boys! Those carrot chunks could break someone's tooth. Smaller! Much smaller!"

Hearing this side of her makes me realize where Sherman got his reputation. So many things come naturally to a family that spends a lot of time together. Being tough works when there is love underneath. And loving means doing the hard work of staying the course.

I questioned coming here, but now I couldn't be more positive that it's exactly where I ought to be.

32

MACK

ONE MORE ROOM.

I square my shoulders as I adjust my Santa sack. I can do this.

Janea, the children's hospital social worker who has served as my guide all morning, glances back, her black braids swinging. "This one might not wake up to talk to you. But her mom asked us to come anyway."

We continue down the hall, past giant photographs of smiling children, some with no hair, others in wheel-chairs, always happy and amazingly cute.

This morning has been tough. For once I'm glad for the hair and beard maintaining my persona as the holly jolly one. Twice, I've barely held it together.

This is my second hospital gig, but the first one was a group activity, a dozen children and their caregivers receiving surprise presents in the art room. Despite the IV stands and wheelchairs, they were boisterous, happy kids.

The children today have been too sick to leave their

rooms. Even so, they've sat up and received their presents. Some got to hug me.

This one might be different.

"Here we are," Janea says. We pause outside the door. "I'll have to ask you to suit up for this one. Normally we wouldn't allow it, but this is a special case."

"I understand."

She opens a cabinet built into the wall and extracts paper scrubs. "I hope I have something big enough for Santa," she says, and I'm amazed that she can laugh. I'm not sure how I will even manage a *ho ho ho* when we go in.

"Here we go," she says. "Extra-extra-large."

"Sounds like Santa's size."

She guides my arm through each side and ties me off in the back. Mega-sized gloves go over my white ones. Then she kneels and fits elastic covers over my shoes.

"We'll leave the bag out here. I'm afraid the fur picks up a lot of dust and germs."

"Not a problem."

She fits a mask over my face, digging through the hair until she finds my ears, then steps back to contemplate my Santa hat. "I don't think I have anything that's going to cover that."

"I can take it off."

"I hate to do that. It's such an important part of Santa." She opens one of the paper hats. "Maybe if I put two together."

She rips the sides of two hats and works on my head. I bend over to make it easier for her.

"There you are. Just don't shake."

"Gotcha." I extract the last gift from my bag. The label on it reads *Calinda Hocking*.

Janae knocks on the door, hesitates a moment, then opens it.

I grip the package in front of me, gathering a laugh in my belly that I can push out no matter what I see in there.

"Santa is here!" Janae says in a singsong. "Calinda, are you ready to see Santa?" She steps aside to give me room to walk in.

I could not have prepared for what I find. The small figure is barely a speed bump on the bed surrounded with monitors and wires and equipment. The room smells of cleaning solution, and the whirs and beeps of machines are intense.

But there are no tubes in her mouth, only a cannula for oxygen fitted to her nose.

A petite woman in a Christmas sweater approaches the opposite side of the bed. "Hello, Santa, I'm Calinda's mom. Let me see if she'll wake up."

I'm not sure what to do, so I stand at the foot of the bed. Calinda has only sprigs of hair that make tight curls around a long bandage over her head.

The mother looks up at me. "She hasn't come out of the surgery as well as we expected. She flits in and out of semi-consciousness." She gazes down on her child with a measure of love that makes my knees weak. "We had you come just in case. We wanted to see if she would wake up enough to talk. If anyone can do it, Santa can."

I grip the present with tight fingers and let out a long, slow exhale. The woman's voice hasn't even wavered. I can't trust mine now.

"Calinda," Mom says. "It's Santa."

The girl draws in a deeper breath.

"That's right," Mom says. "Wake up for Santa!"

"Should I do a big ho, ho, ho?" I ask.

"A really big one," Mom says.

"Ho, ho, ho! Merry Christmas, Calinda!"

For a moment, I don't think it's going to work, but then her eyes flutter open.

"Santa Claus," she whispers.

Mom tries to control her emotion. "You're awake!"

"Santa," Calinda says again.

I step forward. "Santa's right here." Her eyes move my way. "It's Christmas Eve. I have your present!"

She lifts her hand to point at me. "You're wearing paper."

"Well, it's a secret I'm here. It's my disguise." She smiles for a moment, and my chest gets tight. I can't tell for sure her age. Maybe six? Maybe eight? "I'm told you've been a very good girl."

"I think so." Her smile is fleeting, as if it takes great effort, but her eyes stay on me. "Are you the real Santa?"

Despite skirting the issue a dozen times a day at the mall, I change my tune today. "I am." At this point, I'll produce Rudolph if she asks. I'm that determined. "I came here for you."

"Really?"

I nod. "Just for you, Calinda."

She seems to think for a moment, then asks, "Did you park your sleigh on the roof?"

I point to the window. "My sleigh is hidden in the parking garage. Don't tell anyone."

Another fleeting smile. "I won't."

"Would you like me to open the present for you?" her mother asks.

"Yes," Calinda says.

I pass the gift to Mom. I have no idea what this child has asked for, if this is a generic gift or if it has come from a list. I'm handed the presents at these events. They are purchased by volunteers. But I hope with all of the Santa magic in my heart that it is exactly the thing she wants.

Mom tears away the wrapping. Calinda's eyes seem brighter as she watches.

Never has a gift caused me more stress in my life.

"Oh, look!" Mom says, turning the box around.

Inside is an American Girl doll with long hair and a fancy velvet dress.

"Is it her?" Calinda asks.

Mom nods. "It's her."

The little girl's eyes get as big as I've seen them since I walked into the room. "Thank you, Santa! We tried to get one last year but no one had them."

Mom's laugh is shaky. "We went to the store in Los Angeles. We tried online. We even tried bidding on eBay. But we never got one."

Mom takes a moment to extract the doll from the box. I bend down close to the girl. "Merry Christmas, Calinda."

"Merry Christmas, Santa," she says. Her mom passes her the doll. Calinda holds it out in front of her, then brings it to her chest. "It's the best, most perfect present for the best Christmas ever."

"It's a good one," Mom says. She sits down next to her daughter and looks at the doll with her.

A nurse comes in. "I hear somebody's talking!" She moves to the side of the bed. "Excuse me, Santa! It's my turn!"

"Merry Christmas!" I tell Calinda. "Enjoy your doll!"

"I will!"

Janea follows me out to the hall. "What a lovely last visit. Thank you so much for coming. What a blessing."

"Will she be okay?" I know she can't tell me medical information, but I have to ask.

"She's looking better," Janea says. "She gave us a scare." She helps me peel off the paper scrubs.

"It must be so hard spending Christmas in the hospital," I say, bending down to remove the shoe covering.

"It's not the hardest things these families face," she says.

I know what she's saying. My mother was so sudden, so unexpected. None of us got to see her. The baby was born, and then Mom's blood pressure plummeted. She began bleeding out. They rushed her to surgery, and that was it.

None of us were there. Tanya and I were at home watching all the other kids. Dad arrived the next day with baby Betty Sue, and that was when we found out our mother would not be coming home.

"I don't know how they do it," I say. "How they face this day after day."

Janae crumples the scrubs and drops them into a trash bin built into the wall. "One thing these families have taught me is that even when you know hard days are coming, you can still enjoy the right now."

My heart thunders to my shoes. She's right. A difficult path doesn't mean it can't be happy while you're living it.

"Thank you for that," I tell her. "Merry Christmas."

"Merry Christmas, Santa. Do you know your way out?"

"I do." I pick up my empty velvet bag and head to the parking garage, where I indeed parked my mode of transportation. But as I sit behind the wheel, the air conditioning blowing on my face, I can't get past what I've just learned.

Find joy in the ride, no matter how difficult.

Before I can talk myself out of it, I pick up my phone and text Rory.

Merry Christmas. I miss you. I hope to be able to talk to you on Christmas Day. Love, Mack.

And for the first time since our fight, I feel a little lighter.

33

RORY

THE PICKLES HAVE A RIDICULOUSLY LONG TABLE, AS IF serving a feast is always part of the plan. It easily seats the fourteen of us once we're joined by Martin and Fran. Their Christmas Eve tradition begins with an enormous midday meal.

With all the noise of multiple conversations going on, it's easy to focus on the few people near me and not get overwhelmed by too much attention. Sunny is hilarious, always creating unexpected mixtures of expressions to keep everyone in stitches.

"And I told him he was getting too dumb for his britches!" she says, and everyone nearby laughs. "You only get one chance to make a third impression."

I smile to myself. This gathering feels more like a friend circle, people who have chosen to be together, than family. My uncle Thomas would certainly try to crack jokes, but they mostly fell flat in front of my mother, who would fix a beady glare on him. Aunt

Barbara is a giggler, but I never felt the urge to laugh with her. Maybe I feared my mother's disapproval.

This is so different from how I would be spending the day in Palm Springs.

"So, Rory," someone says, and I look down the line to locate the speaker. It's Fran. Aunt Fran, I guess. "Did I hear you used to live in Boston?"

Now the table quiets. Everyone wants to hear about the stranger.

I swallow my bite of potato soufflé. Grammy was right—it's sinfully good. "I did. The first firm that hired me out of law school was in Boston. I stayed there for six years before I became a partner at the Los Angeles firm."

"Will you stay in California, then?" she asks.

All eyes are on me, the eating paused for the moment. Do they really care where I am?

My brain tells me to redirect, to avoid the cross-examination. But for some reason, my mouth spouts the honest answer. "I'm not sure. I interviewed with a Manhattan firm yesterday."

The table erupts in talk.

"She might move to New York!"

"Aren't there spare bedrooms here?"

"Grammy has a spare in Brooklyn, too."

"It would be so good for Sherman to have someone with him again."

Whoa. They're planning my whole life. I can't even pick out who is saying what, it's coming so fast.

"Who's the Pickle lawyer? She could take over the account."

"Isn't one of Patricia's cousins a real estate agent? They could find her a place."

Sherman finally stands up and whistles loudly with his fingers between his teeth. "Now, hold on. Rory's a grown woman. She doesn't need a big ol' Pickle intervention."

The room quiets again. I have a feeling I'm not the only one who wonders if this means he doesn't want to be involved if I move here. This time, my brain obeys me. I straighten my spine and keep my expression carefully neutral.

"Thank you so much for your enthusiasm," I say. "I won't know for a while if anything will happen at all. I could be staying right where I am." I'm already regretting saying as much as I did.

"What about Mack?" Anthony asks. "Isn't he based in Los Angeles, too?"

"Who's Mack?" Fran asks.

"Her…" Anthony trails off. He doesn't know what to call Mack. I don't help him out. I wouldn't know what to say. Former lover? Recent ex? He's not even taking my calls right now, but I don't need to add that detail.

"We met him in L.A." Max has the decency to look uncomfortable that they are bringing my relationship status into the conversation. "He seemed like a great guy."

Fran seems to decide he's a person of interest, so she keeps the inquiry going. "Are you two an item?"

We're something, that's for sure. But everyone's waiting for an answer. Evasion is the only way out. "I'm not sure about Mack's plans."

But then the talk starts all over again.

"Will he move here, too?"

"We should give Shelley the heads-up so she can find an apartment."

"Two people with Sherman would be even better!"

I glance down at Sherman. He has his head down, focusing hard on the piece of ham he's cutting. This is uncomfortable for him. I know exactly how he feels.

Max takes over the talk and directs it away from me. I try to relax. I should have known my life would be too interesting to avoid dissection.

Soon the table is divided by conversation again, and I can focus back on my plate. My new plan is to answer any question with a request for an exhaustive, no-step-removed explanation on how to prepare every single dish at the table.

I needn't have worried. The family has moved on. Soon the meal has wound down and cleanup chores are divvied up, with Sherman and Grammy exempted, since they did the majority of the cooking.

I'm assigned dish drying next to Anthony's washing and Max's repacking of the china and crystal.

"I'm sorry things got out of hand at dinner," Anthony says. "That was my fault."

Max takes a plate from me. "Bro, you gotta stop sticking your nose in Rory's love life."

Anthony dunks another plate in the suds. "I had a long, terrible period on the outs with Magnolia, and I sympathize with anyone going through the struggle."

Max opens the lid on a storage box. "What makes you assume Rory and Mack are struggling?"

"They aren't together at Christmas," Anthony says. "Rory's looking for a job on the opposite side of the country. Obviously, it's about to go south, if it hasn't already."

I accept a wet plate. "I'm right here, you know." I try to keep my voice light, but there's an edge to it.

"See, you're pissing her off," Max says.

"He's not pissing me off," I counter.

"You sound like you're pissed off," Max says.

"You do," Anthony says.

I run a towel along the face of the plate. "I'm avoiding everyone in California. The interview came at a convenient time. That's all."

"Avoiding everyone?" Max asks. "Does that mean your mother?"

"And Mack?" Anthony adds.

I shrug, passing the plate to Max. "When I came to Boston the first time, I left Mack behind. History is repeating itself."

"That would do it," Anthony says. "He's losing you again." He shakes his head, staring into the sink.

"Don't be like that," Max says. "Rory's gotta do what Rory's gotta do."

"I'm not feeling good about my L.A. firm," I say. "It's clear the other partners liked the *idea* of a woman partner more than the reality of having a woman as a partner."

Max freezes in the middle of sliding a plate into the corrugated slot. "Did they do something to you? I will fuck them up."

"No, no," I say quickly. I can see Max smashing the

conference room table with his bare hands. "They've been condescending, as if they have their place at the firm, and I have mine. It's not the way it should work. And if I can't play to their politics, I need to move on."

"There's nothing in L.A.?" Anthony asks.

"I've only begun to think about a change. This opportunity landed in my lap."

"The best ones do," Max says.

Anthony resumes washing his stack. "And Mack knows."

"I told him," I say.

He hands me another plate. "How did he take it?"

"Not great. We haven't spoken since."

Max's face if full of concern as he accepts another plate from me. "How long has it been?"

"Five days."

The two of them look at each other.

"That's too long," Max says. "Do you want to talk to him?"

"Of course. I went to his house. I tried visiting him at…" I hesitate. They don't know Mack is a mall Santa. "I went to his work, but he wasn't there."

"Is he avoiding you?" Anthony has given up on the dishes and leans on the counter, watching me.

"He has to be. We used to text every day, even if we didn't see each other." It's nice to be able to confess to someone. I could never tell any of this to my mother. And I didn't want to admit my love life disaster to Jerome.

Anthony dries his hands. "This can wait. Where's your phone?"

"In my purse." I gesture to my dress. "No pockets."

"So you haven't checked it all day?" Anthony seems shocked.

"Not since I got here."

"Good God," he says, pushing me toward the door. "Surely he won't ignore you on Christmas Eve."

"I don't know why today would be any different." We head through the living room and back to the foyer.

Sherman spots us. "You guys aren't ditching the cleanup already, are you?"

"Showing Rory where we put her things." Anthony moves us to the closet near the door. It's stuffed with coats and bags. "Which one is yours?"

I pull my purse forward from where it hangs on the same hook as my coat. "I'm telling you, he's done."

But when I unlock my phone, there's a message.

"Aha," Anthony says. "I'm never wrong."

Magnolia pauses in the next room where she's rolling up the tablecloth. "Should I remind you of all the times you've been wrong?"

Anthony holds up a hand as if to ward off a deluge of reminders. "What did he say?"

I have to bite my lip a moment to make sure my voice won't waver when I read it aloud. "'Merry Christmas. I miss you. I hope to be able to talk to you on Christmas Day. Love, Mack.'"

Max peers around the doorway to the foyer. "Any word?"

"He misses her," Anthony says. "And he used the word *love*."

Magnolia comes up. "Has he used the word *love* before?"

I shake my head. I can't speak.

"That's it," Anthony says. "We have to get you to L.A."

I shake my head more vigorously.

"Why not?" Max says. "You can make it!"

I clear my throat, trying to pull myself together. "He's in Alabama."

"That's right!" Anthony says. "The nine brothers and sisters."

Jason pops into the foyer. "Y'all ditched the dishes." He sees us all standing around my phone. "Is something going on?"

"Mack and Rory split," Magnolia says. "But he wrote her. And he used the word *love* for the first time."

"First time?" Jason asks.

"First time," Anthony says.

"We have to get her to him," Jason says.

"That's what we're saying!" Anthony says. "But he's in Alabama."

"Call Dell," Jason says. "It's a long shot, but maybe he hasn't gotten there yet. He'll be taking the jet."

"He was in town this morning." Sherman's voice is deeper than the rest and resonates in the small space. "You might catch him."

"Call!" Anthony says. "Somebody, call!"

The next twenty minutes are a blur. Dell is on the tarmac, but his pilot Starr is late, which is typical, apparently, so they can wait another half-hour, since they'll have to adjust the flight plan anyway.

I'm pushed into an SUV, Sherman at the wheel, the brothers around me, assuring me they'll handle my hotel room and my bags. "Buy a toothbrush when you get there," Anthony says.

We drive out onto the airstrip, squealing to a stop not far from a sleek private jet. I barely get to say goodbye to the men before I'm heading up a steep set of stairs into the belly of the plane.

A tall, lean man in a perfectly tailored suit waits at the top. "Welcome, Rory," he says. "I'm Dell Brant." He turns to the space. There's a couple of swivel chairs and two rows of lush padded seats.

A woman sits at a table on the opposite wall, a young girl across from her. They are playing Candyland. She's pregnant, her red dress stretching across her belly.

"That's my wife Arianna, our daughter Grace, and one on the way. I apologize that we don't have any cabin service. It's Christmas Eve, of course. We'll only have a pilot. She doesn't celebrate the holiday."

"Strap in!" comes a voice from the cockpit. "Time to go!"

"So lovely to meet you," Arianna says. "Let me get Grace settled." She straps the little girl into a belt on her seat.

"You and I can take the swivels," Dell says. "I didn't expect to be picking up a passenger this close to Santa's hour."

Grace perks up at that, her eyes big. "He's bringing me a new bicycle!"

"Yes, it will be interesting getting home," Dell says.

"We would have waited until morning, but I don't enjoy traveling on the big day."

"I hope that bicycle's assembled," Arianna says. "Or it will be super interesting."

"Santa's elves will do it," Grace says. "You don't have to worry."

"Indeed," Dell says. He adjusts his seatbelt. "All settled, Rory?"

I nod. I realize I have my coat on and my purse around my shoulder. I drop both to the floor and fasten my buckle.

The lights dim as the plane begins to taxi. Grace stares out the window. "I bet we see Santa on the way."

"I hope not," Arianna says. "If he knows you're awake, he might skip you!"

"I know what to do," Grace says, plunking her head to the table. She pretends to snore.

Arianna and Dell exchange a look of amusement that makes my heart tilt. I should have been spending more time with families all along. I've learned mountains of subtext in only a few days.

We're all quiet as the plane moves into the sky. Grace pops her head up. "Gum, Mommy!"

"Oh, yes," Arianna says. She digs in a bag.

"Now, Mommy!"

Dell pulls a pack from his pocket. "Heads up!" The gum sails across the plane to Grace.

She misses the catch, but it lands on the table, and she sticks a piece in her mouth.

I swallow to pop my ears. I can't believe I'm on a plane to Alabama.

When we've leveled out, Dell heads to a door at the rear of the compartment, returning with bottles of water for everyone. He passes one to me. "I have stronger things in the back," he says. "Just say the word."

"I'm good, thank you," I say.

"So what brings you to the South on Christmas Eve?" Dell asks. "Jason didn't elaborate, only that it was urgent you get there."

"I…" I have no idea what to say.

Arianna glances over. "Don't be nosy, Dell."

"Of course. Forget I asked."

I'm off the hook. But he *did* let me on his plane.

"My…" Oh, what *do* I call Mack? My life has been totally turned upside down, over and over, since December began. But who he is to me should come more easily.

"The love of my life is in Alabama. We had a disagreement before I came to New York. I thought we were done, but then he texted me."

"So it's a love mission!" Arianna says. "How wonderful!"

"We're going to fly into Birmingham," Dell says. "Where is his family?"

"Tuscaloosa. Jason arranged for a car to pick me up and drive me. I understand it's only an hour."

"Good," Dell says. "Sounds like you're all set."

"Do you know what you're going to say?" Arianna asks.

"No," I say.

"Does he know you're coming?" Dell asks.

"No."

"You simply must tell us how this turns out," Arianna says. "I'll give you my number. We can always take you back with us to New York."

"I'll probably go straight back to L.A."

She nods. "I still want to hear the story."

I grip my water bottle tightly. I can only hope it's going to have a happy ending.

34

MACK

I'm relieved that Tanya arrives early.

When my eldest sister knocks on the door of the house I've rented for a few days, I'm up to my shins in tinsel. I manage to untangle myself without tripping and get to the door.

Her hair is in rollers, her dress on a hanger, and she looks ready for serious work in shabby sweats and sneakers.

She glances around, nodding. "Mack, I knew you would not be able to manage this on your own."

"I'm used to having a bit more help."

Tanya hangs her dress on the door of the coat closet and drops her bags. "It's Tuscaloosa on Christmas Eve. The college kids are gone. Anybody willing to work was hired already. Everyone else is with their families."

In L.A., you can generally hire anybody for anything at any time. But I haven't been in Tuscaloosa since I was eighteen years old, other than for my grandmother's funeral. I forgot how different it is.

Tanya circles the living room. "What's the situation? What are we eating? Where are we sitting? Are you going to decorate that tree yourself?"

"I picked up all the catered food an hour ago. It's staying warm in the oven." I head to the kitchen. "I assumed the pies and bread would be fine sitting out."

"What kind of pies?" Tanya peers through the bags. "Chocolate pie should be in the fridge. Fruit pie is fine sitting out. Dang, Mack, you could feed an army with all this."

"It's a lot of people."

"It is. We haven't gotten together since I don't know when." She opens the oven. "A turkey *and* a ham?"

"I thought people could take leftovers. There's a bunch of plastic baggie things in the pantry."

She laughs, and suddenly decades fall away. We're teenagers in our kitchen at home, trying to figure out how to feed everybody.

"Mack, you were a perfectly competent human being when you left home. We used to feed a family of eleven between homework and bedtime. You know what Ziplocs are."

She's right. Somewhere along the way, I chose to become incompetent at household chores and hire it out. Time to step up.

"There's foil and plastic wrap and Ziploc bags," I say. "Between that and the containers everything came in, I think we have it covered."

"That's better," she says. She starts opening cabinets. "Plenty of plates. Hopefully there's enough silverware."

"I bought some paper plates and plastic silverware as backups."

"Good plan. Nobody's going to want to wash all this."

She's right. "I guess I should keep it simple or they'll all complain."

Tanya juts her hip out and crosses her arms over her faded sweatshirt. "Mack, this is the most luxurious Christmas any of us have had, probably ever. You're making this happen. No one will criticize you."

"I'm not sure about that. It's been a twenty-year absence."

"Nobody stayed past graduation. We weren't exactly the Brady Bunch."

That's true. We were a mess before Mom died, and a bigger mess after.

"So what should we do now?" I ask. "We'll want to carve that turkey and ham and make sure it's easy to serve. And the tree isn't done."

Tanya leans over the bar to peer into the other room. "At least it's pre-lit. I say we let everyone decorate the tree together. That'll give them something to do rather than sit around and stare at each other."

"That's smart."

Tanya pokes her forehead. "Somebody had to take charge all those years."

"And you did great. I'm sorry we haven't talked more in the years since then."

She turns around, leaning against the bar. "Mack, you've been carrying a lot of guilt about leaving after high school. But you shouldn't."

"You didn't get to leave."

"I had nowhere else to go. I wasn't college material like you and Georgia. I didn't have the grades to get a scholarship. I just had to keep a roof over my head until I found someone to get me out of there. That's what I did."

"Are you happy with Ridge?"

"Perfectly so. And Juliet is a doll. You saw that yourself."

My chest constricts at the mention of Tanya's daughter. "I still feel bad about what I said at the funeral."

"Think nothing of it. It did my heart good to see the way she handled it."

"You raised a perfect child."

Tanya snorts. "Don't tell her that. She'll think she can get away without eating broccoli." She walks over to the boxes of ornaments and the garland that tangled me earlier. "All this Christmas stuff isn't going to organize itself."

We work companionably for a while, stacking boxes of ornaments on the coffee table and winding the long strands of tinsel to make it easier to put them on the tree. That done, we head to the kitchen to manage the food.

There's a lot to do, but working beside Tanya feels like old times. We carve up the turkey and the ham and place the slices as artfully as we can inside the aluminum containers. Keep it simple, I keep reminding myself. This is about food and family, not looking like Martha Stewart designed it.

When the kitchen is tamed, Tanya disappears upstairs to get dressed.

I try not to be nervous. These are my siblings. I grew up with them.

But I never came back. I know some words are going to be said. And Betty Sue and Aurora were small when I left. Kindergarten and first grade. They might have notions about me that don't hold up.

My mind turns to Rory. In all the craziness, I haven't thought too much about my message to her from this morning. The hospital in California seems a world away. Since then, I've had to fly to Tuscaloosa, rent a car, find the restaurant for the food, and pick up a mountain of wrapped gifts I shipped ahead of time.

It's been a heck of a day, and the evening is still ahead.

I check my phone, abandoned on the counter in the kitchen. Nothing from Rory. I should've known. She's upset that I ignored her, as she should be. She came by the house. My security camera notified me of someone arriving several days ago, and I saw her.

And the receptionist told me she stopped by work. She was trying, and I refused to acknowledge it.

I screwed up. There's no reason to think that a simple text message could fix things. I overreacted. Now I'm paying the price.

I unlock the phone and hover over the keys, thinking I'll write her again. But I did say I wanted to talk to her on Christmas Day, and it's only Christmas Eve. I shouldn't push.

I tuck the phone in my pocket. Tomorrow. I'll write her again tomorrow.

There's a knock at the door.

Tanya is still upstairs. Here goes nothing. If my siblings have something to say about me not coming to see them all these years, I'll just have to listen. Anything they say will likely be true.

I open the door to Simon, Georgia, and Kaya on the porch.

"Welcome," I say. "Merry Christmas."

Georgia comes in first. She wears a Christmas sweater much like the one I saw this morning on the mom in the hospital room. Her expression is serious, but she manages to say, "Merry Christmas," back to me. It looks like she has something on her mind. I've been stalking her social media to figure out gifts and know she's going through a divorce. She was angry her husband made off with her prized cappuccino machine, so of course I've replaced it.

Simon follows her. He wears a Roll Tide T-shirt with jeans and flip-flops. His ancient laptop has been giving him fits, and he needs it for work. A killer replacement is in his gift. He gives a quick nod as he passes.

"Simon, good to see you."

Kaya leaps into my arms in a fiery hug. "Mack! I didn't get to talk to you at the funeral last year. Thank you for organizing this! I'm so excited to see everybody. I can't believe we haven't done this before!"

Her chatter fills the room and gives me a measure of calm. At least one of my siblings doesn't hate me. I know she is going to die over the Coach bag I got her.

She shows off her knockoffs all over her Instagram and has been saving for the real thing.

Kaya sets her coat on a bench near the door, taking in the scene. She's gussied up in a gold dress and heels. Her dark hair is pulled up into a fancy concoction with sparkling gems. She was ten when I left and always a ray of sunshine in the family.

"Look at this huge tree," she says. "So many lights." She turns to me. "Are we going to decorate it?"

I gesture to the boxes of ornaments on the coffee table. "Feel free to get started. I had to fly in today, so I didn't have a chance to get it done."

Kaya lets out a squeal. "I love it." She waves Georgia and Simon over. "Get over here, you two. Let's decorate this tree."

Watching them, I remember the scraggly plastic Christmas tree we used all the years I lived at home. I'm not sure how old it was when Mom died, but we kept the same one all the way to when I left. It was threadbare and dropped plastic bits every time someone slammed the door. But we had a lot of ornaments, and we could certainly cover it up. It always looked all right. Especially when you turned out the overhead lights and let it glow.

"Simon, break open these boxes," Kaya says. "Georgia, you want to start on the garland? That should go on first."

It's interesting to watch the dynamic, the younger one guiding the others. We older ones bossed the little ones around back in our day. But we're not children anymore. There is no pecking order.

Tanya comes down the stairs.

"Tanya!" Kaya cries, dashing toward her for a hug. "Where's sweet Juliet?"

"She's coming later with Ridge. I came early to help Mack."

"Well, something smells delicious," Kaya says.

There's another knock on the door, so I turn back to it.

It's Dante this time, broad-shouldered and tough in an unbuttoned gray shirt over a white T-shirt. He holds up his fist, and I bump it. "Good to see you, man," he says.

"Good to see you, too." Dante was only nine when I left. The young ones resent me less than the older ones. Probably they had more chores after I was gone.

I can't stop thinking about this. I catch Tanya giving me a look that says, *Get out of your head.*

Busted.

Dante fist-bumps Simon and accepts a hug from Kaya. He and Georgia give each other a nod. There are dynamics within the sibling group that will certainly come to light over the next few hours.

I take one end of the tinsel garland Georgia is stringing and help her get it around the tree. It's about half up when someone else knocks.

"I'll get it!" Kaya calls, and bounds to the door.

This time it's Betty Sue with Aurora in tow. She must've picked Aurora up from the bus station.

"Now the party can start!" Betty Sue hollers, holding up two bottles of whiskey. Her hair is long and loose, huge gold hoops swinging from her ears. She is the smallest of all of us in a red crop top and jeans. I remember when she came home, barely six pounds.

Aurora keeps her head down as she turns and closes the door. She wears one of those big poncho-style shawls, her dark hair trailing down her back. Her eyes dart from side to side as if she hopes no one will notice her.

Kaya hasn't even closed the door when Ian slips through, tall, slender, and studious. The quietest McAllister. He gives us all a nod.

Tanya walks over. "Aurora, I'm so glad you were able to come down." She looks around. "Looks like we're just missing Luke, right? Plus Ridge and Juliet?"

Kaya returns to her ornament station at the coffee table. "Luke was always late."

"So is Ridge!" Dante calls. They laugh, an easy, comfortable sound.

Aurora sits on the sofa in the corner. "I'll watch if that's okay," she says. She arranges the poncho around her.

She's pregnant, but I'm not sure who knows. I uncovered it accidentally when I was stalking her for gifts. One of her friends posted about Aurora's deadbeat baby daddy, who abandoned them when he got the news, and later, the post was deleted.

I guess she's trying to hide her belly as long as possible. I'm certainly not going to say a thing, but I did open a two-thousand-dollar line of credit at the baby store in her town for her. I'll slip her the card in secret later.

"I can get drinks for everyone," I say. "We have

wine. Looks like Betty Sue brought the whiskey. There's also soda and tea."

Betty Sue dumps her purse on the bench. "Mack McAllister, did you just say soda?"

The room erupts in laughter.

"It's Coke, Mack," Kaya says. "Who took the 'Bama out of the boy?"

"He's been assimilated," Simon says, rushing over to rub his fist on my hair.

"Hey, I'm the oldest, I give out the noogies!" I say, barely missing getting him back as he ducks out of my grasp.

This is better.

Betty Sue whistles loudly. "Break it up, ya hooligans. I've got the drinks. What's everybody want? Never mind. You get what I give you!"

I glance over at Aurora. She doesn't seem concerned, so Betty Sue must be in the know. They rode over together, so probably they're tight.

The tree decorating is going well, although Dante only put up a couple of ornaments before dropping into a chair. "Some of us had to work all day," he says.

"Still putting up that house on Fairview?" Kaya asks.

"Got the frame done today. Construction stops for no man, not even baby Jesus."

Betty Sue returns, passing what appears to be whiskey and Coke to her siblings.

Aurora gets one as well, but I catch Betty Sue's wink and Aurora's quick nod of acknowledgment. Hers is probably straight Coke.

"Can't forget you, Mack," Betty Sue says, passing

me a glass. "We're all fancy using actual glassware. Nobody bought any red Solo cups!"

"We'll break half of them before the night's over," Tanya says.

There's another knock at the door, and this time it's Luke, along with Ridge and Juliet. "We drove up at the same time," Ridge says. "Good to see you, Mack."

"Uncle Mack!" Juliet runs to hug me around the waist. "You have the prayer pebble I gave you?"

"Right in my pocket," I say. I flash it quickly, so she won't notice it's not exactly the same as the one she gave me.

"Good." She sees the decorations going up. "Don't put them all up! Wait on me!"

Tanya puts her arm around Ridge and kisses his cheek. "Glad you made it, honey."

"I wouldn't miss this shindig. Not in a fancy house in Riverside."

Tanya leans around him. "Hey, Luke, you're quiet."

"'Sup." Luke drops onto the sofa opposite Aurora and pulls out his phone. I catch Tanya's gaze, and she shrugs.

Speaking of phones, I take mine out to surreptitiously snap photos of all the siblings as they decorate the tree. Betty Sue delivers more booze. Tanya finds the cheese and meat plates and sets them out on the coffee table now that it's empty of ornaments.

Ridge collects the trash from the ornament packaging and bags it up. Their personalities are starting to come through. Betty Sue and Kaya keep the party going. Georgia quietly executes the plans. Luke and

Aurora seem content to sit quietly on the far wall with Ian. Simon and Dante stand in one corner talking, drinking whiskey and Coke.

If only Dad were here. Everyone knows he isn't coming, and Tanya said nobody was likely to bring it up. They only ever saw him if they took him something to eat. He was unwilling to leave the house for this.

Tanya also looked into checking Grandpa out of the nursing home for the evening, but when she got there this afternoon, they said he was having a bad day and to maybe try again tomorrow.

So this is it.

I walk around the room, jumping into conversations. I learn Dante has worked up to being a foreman on his construction sites. Georgia gets to teach an elective this year, and she's stoked about it.

Kaya works as a bank teller, which makes sense. I've never met one who isn't friendly like her. Betty Sue is working at a bar. She has the temperament for that kind of work and enjoys telling stories about her worst customers.

Tanya pronounces the food ready to eat, and we pile into the kitchen to fill our plates buffet-style. The table seats eight, which was about as good as I could do in a rental, but everyone spreads out on the sofas and chairs.

Betty Sue makes another round of drinks, and the chatter gets easier. Even Luke contributes a sentence or two.

This is how Christmas ought to be.

35

RORY

When the car pulls up to a ramshackle house in a run-down neighborhood, the driver says, "I don't think I should leave you here until you confirm with me that you're going to be okay."

It's dark, and only a few houses on the street have Christmas lights up.

I know from conversations with Mack that his dad still lives in their childhood house. I've flown here on the assumption that this is where he is meeting his family.

But given it's Christmas Eve and all the lights are out, I have a feeling I got it wrong. Either that or the party is already over.

I'm about to tell the man to drive me to a hotel, so I can contact Mack rather than surprise him, when a light comes on.

"How about I knock on the door, and if everything is okay, I'll wave to you," I say. "Thank you for looking out for me."

He nods. "Not a problem."

He's a nice man. We chatted on the route from Birmingham to Tuscaloosa. His wife died a few years back, and his kids live in all sorts of far-flung cities. They will be coming to Birmingham in a week to celebrate a late Christmas, so he's making the most of the spare time trying to earn money. He was grateful for this gig. It's a hefty fare to drive this long a route.

I step out onto the cracked sidewalk. The lawn hasn't had actual grass in years, by the looks of it. The lone streetlight at the corner helps me pick my way to the front door.

Obviously, Mack's family isn't here, but whoever is home might know what hotel he's staying at. I might have to accept that there will be no Christmas surprise. It will be just as happy, I hope. Surely he won't turn me aside after flying all this way.

Pressing the bell does nothing, so I rap on the door. It occurs to me for the first time that Mack himself may not know where his dad lives. Maybe since the funeral a year ago, he's gone somewhere else. Anything could've happened.

I wait a while, but no one comes to the door.

I knock again, this time calling out, "Hello? I'm Mack's girlfriend."

The word feels foreign to me. I might have used it easily back in law school, but now it seems so youthful, the wrong description of what Mack and I are to each other. But I have to say something.

A shuffling step approaches from the other side of the thin door. "Who did you say?" The voice is gruff and unfriendly.

"I'm Rory Sheffield. Mack's girlfriend. I thought he was going to be here on Christmas Eve."

The door opens. The old man stands tall in his threadbare bathrobe, flattened slippers unlikely to provide much cushion in his walk.

He peers at me, squinting. "Nobody told me Mack had a girlfriend."

"When did you speak to him last? I'm pretty recent. Well, recent this time. We dated in law school."

"I might've heard about that," he says. "But it doesn't matter. He's not here. They're all having a party in some highfalutin place that Mack rented. I'll sit here with my thoughts if it's all the same to you."

"You don't want to be with your children on Christmas? This is the first one Mack has been back for in twenty years."

"Like I said, I'd rather be here with my thoughts."

He starts to close the door, but I press my hand against it. "Can you tell me where they are? He doesn't know I'm coming. I'm a surprise."

He sniffs. "Beats the hell out of me. I quit listening when they said they were going to be over in the hoity-toity neighborhood. Like this one isn't good enough for him."

Oh. Now I see. Mack didn't ask his dad where to have the gathering, and he's insulted.

Time to be the lawyer I know I can be. "Mr. McAllister, are you standing in front of me saying that if your son had asked you if you could use this house to host a last-minute Christmas party for a dozen people, you would've been fine with that?"

"Well, I—"

"And furthermore, are you suggesting that because he decided to host it at a place that would not require any effort on your part for cleaning or decorating, where you could simply come and enjoy the company of your family, that it is somehow worse? That this is something you should be disgruntled about?"

"I didn't think of it that way—"

"And on top of that, can you imagine the shadow that has been cast over the gathering because you're not there? Do you want that on your conscience? The first Christmas everyone gets together, and you're being a stubborn old Scrooge."

"You don't need to insult me."

"I'm informing you that your behavior impacts their Christmas, too. They want you there. So I'm here to take you."

"Lady, where are you from? I can tell it's not from around here. Do you even have a car?"

I gesture to the black SUV waiting by the curb. "As good as Cinderella's carriage. You want to go in your robe, or do you want to get dressed?"

Giving people two options makes it harder for them to say no to both.

"Just give me a damn second," he says. He shuffles back inside the house.

"I will let the driver know we will be a moment."

Mack's dad waves his hand to acknowledge he's heard me.

I hurry back down the walk. The driver rolls down the passenger window.

"We're going to be taking Mack's dad to the new location, is that okay by you? I can pay you extra."

He holds up his hand. "I got paid plenty for this gig. Happy to take you wherever you need to go."

"Thank you."

Then I'm back to the house. The door creaks as I push inside. I can hear drawers opening and closing in a room toward the back.

So this is Mack's family home. I snap on the front light. Only one yellow bulb illuminates the dusty room.

There's a sagging sofa covered in a faded quilt. An old TV stand holds a relatively recent television. The recliner has towels on the arms and the back, and a small side table next to it is covered with Kleenex and pill bottles.

Mack's dad is used to being alone.

Not tonight. Not if I can help it.

On the far wall is a line of photographs. The first one shows a young Mr. McAllister with a pretty wife and a baby girl, who I assume is Tanya.

With each progressive photo, another child is added.

But there are only nine photos. The frames are off-center on the wall, as if someone moved them in anticipation of a new family photo that would include the tenth baby. But the photo was never taken.

I watch as Mack ages. They weren't dressed fancy, but they all seem healthy and clean and happy. They got by. Until they didn't.

Mr. McAllister returns to the living room. "You think this will do?"

He's wearing a white button-down shirt and a pair

of brown slacks. He swapped out his house shoes for a pair of wrinkled loafers.

"You look fantastic," I say. "Will you do the honor of escorting me to meet your family?"

He lets out a harrumph, but takes my arm in his as we leave the house and lock the door.

Only then do my knees decide to go weak with what I'm about to do.

Mr. McAllister peers out the window at the house we pull up to. He was joshing me earlier. His daughter Tanya wrote the address on a piece of paper.

He whistles low. "Look at this place. Does Mack own it or something?"

I lean down to look. "There's a website where you can rent houses. He got it for a few days to host the gathering. Makes it easier on everyone."

The driver opens Mr. McAllister's door and helps him out. I press my bag against my hip as I step onto the sidewalk. I have nothing but my coat and my purse, but Max's watch is tucked inside. I didn't want to leave such a pricey item in the hotel when I left for the Pickles'. Now I'm glad.

I take Mr. McAllister's arm. "Thank you," I say to the driver. "Have a lovely visit with your family next week."

He gives a bow. "I will."

The house is ablaze with lights. Mack must have asked the owners to decorate, or perhaps they did it on their own. It looks beautiful. It's two stories and sprawls on a large lawn with giant trees shading either side.

"The electric bill must be terrific," Mr. McAllister says.

"I bet so."

We take our time moving up the walk. When we get to the door, Mr. McAllister stands tall and pushes the doorbell.

Inside, I hear music and lots of laughing. The party is still going on.

The door flies open, and a woman in a red dress looks at us in surprise. "Dad?" She looks at me. "Are you Rory?"

"I am. I picked up a passenger on the way here."

She looks from her dad to me and back again. "Does Mack know you're coming?"

I shake my head.

The woman turns to the room. "Look, everyone, Dad made it!"

Several people shout a greeting, and a little girl runs up and hugs him around the waist. "Granddad! I was hoping you would come!"

Mr. McAllister places his hand on her small head. He glances up at me, and I nod in acknowledgment that he's glad he came.

Me, I'm not so sure yet.

"I'm Tanya," the woman says, leading us into the expansive living room. There are people everywhere, filling both sofas, on chairs, on the floor, on barstools next to the kitchen. A Christmas tree is loaded with decorations. It smells of food and whiskey and wine.

I search among the faces, but Mack isn't among them.

"This is Rory, everyone," Tanya announces. "She's Mack's girlfriend. Apparently Mack doesn't know she's coming."

"Hide her!" a late-twenties woman with long, dark hair says. "We can surprise him!"

Tanya turns to me. "Is it a good idea? Will that work?"

It will definitely have the element of surprise. "I think so," I say. It might be better to get him blindsided with everyone nearby. As a lawyer, he should be able to hold his reaction together even if he's not happy to see me.

But he did send that message. I have to believe.

Tanya settles her dad in an armchair and gets him a glass of wine. "I'll fix you a plate in a minute," she says. "Mack is about to come down."

The girl, who must be the Juliet that Mack spoke of, sits on the floor near him. "He's going to play Santa. He has presents."

The woman who suggested I hide takes my arm. "Let's put you over here by the tree. He won't be able to see you when he comes down the stairs."

"I have an idea," Tanya says. "Let's turn out all the lights other than the tree, and when he comes down, we will all shine our phone lights on Rory."

Oh boy.

"Yes," the other woman says. "I'm Kaya, by the way. One of the middle sisters."

"Nice to meet you," I say.

She pulls me behind the tree as a resounding "Ho, ho, ho" booms out from the top of the stairs.

I peer from around the tree as Mack comes down in his full Santa regalia. He has a giant red bag stuffed with presents. He's been shopping for weeks for everything, stalking social media of his siblings and putting together ideas from Tanya for all the members of the family.

Juliet stands up and claps. "Uncle Mack! He's the best Santa ever!"

He gets about halfway down the stairs before he pauses. "Why is it so dark down here?"

"Come down and see, Uncle Mack Santa!" Juliet calls.

He finishes his descent and waits at the bottom. "Is there something I should know about?"

I step out from behind the tree. The first phone light hits me, and then a dozen of them are suddenly shining my way.

Mack sets down his bag. "Rory?"

I hold out my arms. "Straight from New York. You said you hoped to talk to me on Christmas. Here I am."

I don't know what I expect him to do. He might be stoic, because of the time we spent apart. Or he could hold himself back, because of the huge audience. Maybe he's not into affection in front of family.

But he rushes forward as if we haven't seen each other for years. And in a moment, I'm in his arms, and he presses my head to his velvet shoulder. "I can't believe you came," he says. "I could never have dreamed it."

The siblings chorus their exclamations of "kiss her" and "where's the mistletoe" and "gross" as he pulls away to look at me.

We have an audience, so I hope my expression tells him I'm sorry I didn't include him in my decisions.

I think he gets it, because he says, "As long as we're together, we can figure it out."

Tears spring to my eyes. He's right. "I think we already are," I say.

He presses his furry face to mine. I have to laugh, because it tickles so much. I can barely find his lips amidst all the fluff.

I pull away. "We can try that again later."

"Yeah!" Juliet says. "Save the mushy stuff for when you're by yourselves."

The room erupts in laughter and clapping.

The light flicks back on and Mack spots his father. "Dad? When did you get here?"

He points to me. "Your woman dragged me here."

Mack squeezes my waist. "Then everything is perfect." He kisses my cheek. "I have lots of gifts. Who's going to help me pass them out?"

Juliet jumps up, her arm in the air. "Me, me, me!"

"Well, step right up," Mack says. "Let's hand out some presents."

As the gifts are passed out, Juliet announcing each recipient before handing them over, I learn the names of this massive family and put them with the faces.

Tough Tanya. Joyous Juliet. Reserved Ridge. Genuine Georgia. Serious Simon. Kind Kaya, who makes everyone feel welcome. Domineering Dante, who reminds me of Max. Lounging Luke, who is buried in his phone the whole time, but looks up when a gift is dropped into his lap. Invisible Ian, quiet and blending in. Overwhelmed Aurora, who stays close to Luke but looks super stressed out.

Then there's Bouncy Betty Sue, the life of the party, passing out drinks and making sure no one frowns for long.

Mr. McAllister presides over everything from his armchair, his eyebrows rising when gifts are dropped into his lap as well.

It's loud. It's all over the place. Some participate. Some don't. Some laugh. Others are serious.

But this is his family.

And maybe, if Mack and I can figure things out, it will also be mine.

36

MACK

When I close the door on the last sibling to leave, Rory is busy picking up cups. She seems nervous, and Rory's never nervous.

Rather than ask about it, I help her, gathering anything left in the living room. I've ditched the Santa outfit, so I tuck all the parts back into their bag. My reign as St. Nick is over for this year.

The place isn't too crazy of a mess. Ridge and Tanya did the bulk of the work, gathering trash from the gifts and loading up the dishwasher with plates and silverware.

Like every family, my siblings include neat freaks and slobs, helpers and slackers. But the room is presentable in no time, and we leave the last stray items in the sink for the morning.

"I assume you're staying here?" Rory asks.

"I am. And I assume you are?"

Rory fiddles with her hair, loose and curly tonight. "I

left in a hurry. My bags are in New York. I don't even have a toothbrush."

"I think I saw some packaged ones up there."

"Good." She looks everywhere in the room except at me. "There didn't seem to be anything open on the route between your father's house and here."

"Not too surprising. We might be able to find a gas station if we have to."

"I can manage a day. The Pickles are going to send my bags down, but it may have to wait until the day after Christmas."

I start to make a quip about her staying naked until then, but only say, "There's a washer and dryer here."

"That's good." She runs her hands along the kitchen counter.

"Everyone is so glad you got Dad to come. Tanya said she tried everything. They even sent a guilt brigade that included Betty Sue, Kaya, and Georgia. But no dice."

Rory picks up a dishtowel and folds it. "I was glad he had the address. I don't know what I would've done if he hadn't."

I take the dishtowel from her and tilt her chin to look at me. "You could have simply texted me."

"I almost did half a dozen times. But Anthony and Max got it in my head that this should be a Christmas surprise. And it was a stroke of luck that their friend was headed to Birmingham with his private plane."

"I wondered how you got here. A private jet?"

"Yep. My first one. Surely you've ridden on one before, with all those fancy celebrities and athletes."

"Nobody's that rich," I say. "There's celebrity rich, and then there's business billionaire rich. Two completely different orders of magnitude."

Rory seems better, so I release her and turn off the light in the kitchen. The downstairs is lit only by the glow of the Christmas tree. We pause at the base of the stairs to look at it. Most of the ornaments are gone, taken by siblings for their trees. I had nothing else to do with them. But even with only lights and garland, it's still beautiful.

"Shall we go upstairs?" I ask her.

"Okay."

She seems shy. I suppose that should seem odd, given our history, two rounds of love affairs with pretty wild sex lives involved.

But I get it. Something feels different now. The argument. The distance. It's so recent.

We walk side by side up the carpeted staircase. There are three bedrooms and two bathrooms up here. Technically, she could have her own if she wanted.

But that's silly. She doesn't. She didn't come all this way to sleep in a spare room.

I lead her to the master bedroom. "You want me to track down that toothbrush for you?"

"In a minute."

She sits down on the end of the bed. The room is enormous, with a vaulted ceiling and a reading nook that looks out on the water.

Rory seems small sitting there in her green dress, her black curls flowing over her shoulders. She kicked off her heels hours ago, and one bare foot rests on top of the other.

I lean against the doorframe. "Are you all right? You're bound to be tired. It was quite a journey."

"You too. You were at a hospital in Los Angeles this morning. Then you hosted a party in Alabama."

We're talking circles around the real issue. I'll be patient. She has to be here for a reason. You don't fly away from two families of your own to spend Christmas with strangers unless you have something to say.

So I wait.

She draws in a large breath, sitting tall. "I should have mentioned to you the decisions I was making about my career. I know we've only been seeing each other a month, but we have a huge history. So it's really one month plus two years that we've been together."

Now we're getting somewhere. I cross the room and sit next to her on the bed. "You're not used to conferring with others."

"I'm not. I'm very focused. But when you quit talking to me, I realized, finally realized, that there was more that mattered than my career." She cuts her eyes at me. "Or my urges."

I laugh and take her hand. "I like your urges just fine."

"I didn't tell you this mainly because it made me feel vulnerable." She hesitates, her gaze on our joined hands. "During those ten years we were apart, I did try to date other people. But when it came right down to it, I couldn't give myself over to them." She looks me in the eyes. "Do you understand what I'm saying?"

My chest reverberates with shock. "You're saying you didn't sleep with anyone?"

She nods. "As wild as I was when we got back together, it probably seemed like I was all over the place with everyone. But there's a certain level of safety you have to feel to get that crazy. At least for me. I'm sure there are plenty of people who take crazy risks in public places out of sheer wildness, but it isn't that way for me. It comes from safety."

I press my lips into her hair. It smells of fruity shampoo and Christmas dinner. "I would very much like to extend that safety to you again."

"I want that too."

I have to ask the next question. "What about New York?"

"I'm quite sure they will offer the partnership to me. And I definitely want to leave my current firm."

"I see."

She cups the back of my neck. "I can stay in Los Angeles. There are other firms. But I'd like you to look into something for me."

"Anything."

"What will it take to open a second branch of your agency?"

"Be bicoastal?"

"Yes. It's a power position for any lawyer."

I nod. "It can be done. I just have to get licensed in New York."

She draws in a shuddering breath. "This time, I'm asking you to follow me."

Her honey-brown eyes are on mine, searching for my answer.

I get past the lump in my throat and promise her, "I will do that."

"I think I love you, Mack," she says. "Forgive me if I'm a little slow to get it."

I push loose sprigs of hair off her forehead. "I've loved you all this time. Forgive me if I refused to let it go."

She leans into me, and this kiss feels like the first one on that college bench so long ago. Before we fell apart. Before we knew that doors would close. Before we lost each other.

Our future breaks wide open, and our troubled history shifts to the past, as if nothing can ever come between us. We won't let it weigh us down again.

I wake up on Christmas morning with something tickling my chest.

I open my eyes. Rory sits on the bed wearing my Santa beard and mustache and hair, plus the hat.

And nothing else.

"I don't know if I should be freaked out or completely turned on by this," I say.

She lifts the bed covers and peers down at me. "Looks like the answer is *turned on*."

I grab her around the waist and pull her to me. "You are the best Christmas morning gift I could ask for." I kiss her. "Okay, the beard has got to go." The vision of the white, wispy beard touching the tops of her breasts is sending too many jarring signals in my head.

She reaches behind her neck and unties the string. "I didn't glue it on like you do. I'm not crazy."

She sets the beard and hair aside on the nightstand. Now I have her, naked, straddling me.

I'm not letting this go to waste.

I lift her by the waist. "You ready for this?"

"Always."

I aim her carefully above me and bring her down so that I slide directly inside her.

She props her arms on the pillow on either side of my head and shifts up and down on me.

The windows bathe her in golden light. Last night washes over me, the words we said, the decisions we made.

If our love was hushed and reverent last night, this morning it's hot and fevered.

I grasp her waist and increase her pace, making her breasts sway by my face. I lift my head, catching a nipple in my mouth.

She sucks in. "Oh, Mack, here we go." Her movements switch to tiny circles, and she grinds against me.

I love it.

"Jesus, Mack. Oh my God."

I watch the parts of her body that bloom pink from the blood flow, and contractions take over her muscles. She closes her eyes, her lips parted, and then she collapses on me, crying out, laughing, loving every bit of it.

I flip us over, propped on one arm, my face close to

hers. "This will never get old," I tell her.

"Agreed," she says, breathless.

I pound against her, and she lifts her chin to watch my face. She likes to see this part, too.

Sweat gathers on the small of my back. I empty into her, fierce and frenzied. When I'm spent, I turn us to lie face to face on our sides.

Only then do I realize my wrist feels heavy.

I lift it. There's a watch on it. "What is this?"

"Took you long enough to notice. Santa came."

"We sure did."

She smacks my chest.

"Did I ever tell you how my siblings and I would make a list of all the Christmas songs with 'come' in the title?"

"No."

"'O Come, All Ye Faithful.'"

"Mack!"

"'O Come, O Come, Emmanuel.'"

"You're going to hell!"

"'It Came Upon the Midnight Clear.'"

"Stop!"

"'Come and I Will Sing You.'"

"Now you're making them up."

"No! That's a real one!"

She laughs so hard her boobs quiver. "Look at your damn gift, Mack."

I examine the watch. It is handsome and tailored and precise. "I love it. As soon as my athletes see it, it's going to become all the rage."

"Good. I had it engraved."

I open the clasp and slip it over my hand. I aim the back of the watch toward the window so that I can read the words.

Seeing them, I realize that Rory took a risk. She didn't know how our conversation would go when she had these words inscribed. But she had faith.

I run my thumb over them. These words will certainly last forever.

Our time has come.

37

RORY

CHRISTMAS DAY

Once we're finally out of bed, Mack and I take it easy on Christmas morning. We eat leftovers for breakfast and talk about our plans for the rest of the holiday.

Among doing other things, possibly involving chocolate pie eaten somewhere other than a plate.

Around midmorning, I get a text from Anthony. When I see it, I almost drop the phone.

Mack moves next to me, his chin on my shoulder. "What's wrong?"

"My mother is in New York."

"Really?"

I type a text back to Anthony. *When? How?*

His answer is swift. *She regretted how things were left. She's never had a Christmas without you.*

"I think you need to go," Mack says.

"I'm not leaving you alone on Christmas Day."

"I can go with you. Nothing says I have to stay here just because I rented a house."

"Aren't you going to see your family again?"

"You're my family."

He's right. Now that the doors are open, we can come to Alabama whenever we want.

I stare at my phone. "You think we can get a flight?"

"Who brought you here?"

"A friend of the Pickle family. Dell Brant."

Mack's eyebrows shoot to his hairline. "You came here on Dell Brant's private jet?"

"Yeah. Is that a big deal?"

"He's only one of the richest people in the world."

"Should I text him?"

He stares at my phone. "You have Dell's personal phone number?"

"Sure. And his wife's. He's a normal guy. He brought me drinks on his plane, since his usual flight attendant was off for Christmas. The pilot is Muslim, so she was more than happy to fly us."

Mack falls back on the bed. "You're telling me that financial magnate Dell Brant brought you drinks while on his private plane on Christmas Eve."

"Mack. You of all people should know that celebrities and professional athletes and billionaires are regular people."

"Regular people who get everything they want."

"Like you don't."

"I didn't sign Gabby Douglas. And believe me, I tried."

"I'm texting him. All he can do is say no."

"I like the way you think." He clasps his hands behind his head on the pillow. "Fire away. I'll just watch my girlfriend text one of the most powerful men in the Northern Hemisphere."

I text Dell. *Not sure when you were headed back to New York, but my mother went there looking for me. Trying to find a way back.*

I lie next to Mack. "If this doesn't work, I can try commercial airlines."

"You could pull a *Home Alone* and hitchhike with John Candy."

"I think he died when we were teenagers."

"What?" Mack sits up. "Oh, right. I forgot. I hate it when comedians die young."

"I suppose I don't want to spend Christmas Day in an airport trying to nab an empty seat."

"Did you ever think your mom would do that?"

"No way. Although I suppose this is her fault for going to New York without checking if I was there."

He nudges me with his elbow. "Like her daughter showing up in Alabama without checking where I was?"

"Mack Squared, I'm going to get you for that." I straddle his face, knees pinning his arms, and tickle the hell out of his belly.

He laughs for a moment, his mouth full of things his mouth tends to like, then tosses me across the bed. "Payback for that will be hell."

He dives for me.

I'm ready to take my punishment.

Dell's plane didn't work out for the way home, but he did manage to find us a charter that got us to New York by midafternoon.

Mack is only mildly disappointed, since he had plans for what would happen between us alone on a private jet. "We'll make the mile-high club soon enough," he says. "I'm not opposed to commercial flight bathrooms."

"Eww!" I say as we approach the steps to the Pickles' brownstone.

It's different walking up this time. I have Mack by my side. And inside, I'll find my mother.

I don't even have to knock on the door. They've obviously been watching for me. The door flies open and Anthony says, "Rory! Mack! It's like a Christmas miracle."

"It's been a lot of flying in two days," I say.

He steps back. "Come in. Grammy is making a casserole with the leftovers from yesterday."

The house is quieter than before. Fran and Martin, Sunny, Greta, Jude, and little Caden have moved on to other Christmas celebrations.

Nova and Camryn sit chatting on the sofa in the front room. They wave as we come in.

"Everyone's in the kitchen," Nova says.

This time, Anthony remembers to take our coats. We didn't bring much. Mack's bags went to my hotel. My Alabama stay was so short that all my things are still there.

"Did you guys leave a booby trap for Santa?" I ask Anthony.

Anthony grins. "Max did it. Nailed Jason trying to heat up the last serving of Grammy's potato soufflé."

"Where was it?"

"Over the microwave. Classic cup of juice set on top of the door. He opened it and it spilled all over his head." Anthony turns to Mack. "The microwave is over the stove."

"I can picture it," Mack says.

I have to laugh. "You guys are terrible."

"You just wait," Anthony says. "You'll get yours eventually."

Will I? "Should we head to the kitchen?"

Anthony nods. "They're in there."

"This way," I tell Mack.

I lead him to the kitchen door. Jason is busy chopping. Max is at the sink. Grammy Alma peers in the oven window much like she was doing when I saw her the first time.

She turns when she sees me. "Welcome back, Rory."

But what interests me the most is my mother and Sherman, sitting together at a small breakfast table in a nook in the far corner of the kitchen.

Like, *really* close together.

They're so involved in their conversation that at first, they don't even notice us.

I finally clear my throat. "Mom?"

She jumps up from her chair as if she's been caught doing something naughty. "Rory!"

Sherman stands. "This must be the Mack we've heard so much about. Was he worth flying across the country for on Christmas Eve?"

I reach for Mack's hand, curious about what the two of them were up to. "Most definitely."

Mom approaches. She looks completely different than when I saw her last, clutching a bottle of rum at Stringy's Steaks. Her eyes are bright. She seems…happy.

I'm not used to this.

"What's going on here?" I ask.

"I could ask you the same thing," Mom says. "You took off for New York on my holiday."

"I told you I was."

Her laughter is strange, almost girlish. Is she drunk?

"Mom, what have you been doing?"

Sherman approaches. "She arrived early this morning. Waited all night for a chance to get a seat standby."

"I couldn't go a Christmas without seeing my baby," Mom says.

I've never heard her say anything close to those words. "Mom, what's gotten into you?"

She glances at Sherman. "We've been talking. And Sherman has helped me see some things I didn't before."

I still feel suspicious. "What's that?"

"It's a lot," Sherman says. "She's never told anybody."

"Nobody," Mom says. "Not even Grandmom and PawPop."

I squeeze Mack's hand. "Are you going to tell us now?"

She reaches out and presses her hand to my cheek, a show of affection she has never in my life showered on me before. "Not on Christmas Day. It's too sad. Too tragic. But know that I did have a great love once. And my ridiculous idea to live a certain way afterward was a mistake." She turns to Sherman. "Sherman lost his great love, and he has a wonderful life full of family and devotion."

"That must have been some talk," Mack says.

"For another day," Mom says. "For now, I have presents! Can we go open them?"

"Sure," I say, still uncertain.

I feel almost as though I'm living some other life as we all move to the living room, Max convincing Grammy that her casserole can go unwatched for fifteen minutes.

I open gifts from all three of the Pickle brothers—a bright scarf, a pretty pendant necklace, and a soufflé crock Anthony ran out for last minute after I fell in love with Grammy's yesterday.

Mom gives me a lovely long sweater and a photo album hand-crafted with rice paper.

"Open it," she says.

Inside are images that have been on our walls, professional portraits of the two of us in stiff, formal clothes.

But between them are snapshots. Me at the park. Mom and I watching the Olympics, the table covered in paper printouts of the schedule. My kindergarten graduation, which she called a waste of time back in the day. Many of the shots I've never seen before.

"Where did you get these?"

"Grandmom and PawPop. I might be terrible at

sentimental memories, but they had pictures to give me. I had them all printed after that day at the restaurant. I'm trying. I think I'm doing better."

"You're going to be great," Sherman says, and her warm smile at him makes everyone else in the room exchange glances.

I lean into Mack. "Is this weird?" I whisper.

"Maybe?"

"I have something for Rory," Sherman says. He seems different from yesterday. Being around my mother must have done something to him, too. He hands a package over. "We had to work with what we had on hand, but Grammy is good at the needle."

Grammy practically beams. "It's from me too, but it was Sherman's idea."

I pull off the wrapping and open the box.

Inside is a green T-shirt that reads, *Manhattan Pickle. Austin Pickle. L.A. Pickle. Boulder Pickle.* I flip it over. On the back is a list of names. Sherman Pickle. Jason Pickle. Max Pickle. Anthony Pickle.

Hand-stitched at the bottom is another name. *Rory Pickle.*

"But she's a Sheffield," Mom interjects.

Sherman shakes his head. "Every Pickle's a Pickle."

38

MACK

I take Rory's hand as we walk the hall of the UC Berkeley's Alumni House. Light from the wall of windows makes her shimmery gold dress sparkle as she moves. Her riotous hair is down, the way I like it best. Although, I admit, I do enjoy taking it down from an updo to have it spill across my pillow.

"So who ended up registering?" Rory asks.

"Jenessa for sure. Henry, of course. And Marta."

"It will be like the gang all getting together," she says.

"Except we're old now."

Rory shoves me in the shoulder. "Who are you calling old? I'm not the one turning forty next year."

"Only two years for you." I give her a wide grin.

The noise levels increase as we approach the event room. Registration is set up outside the open doors, and a huge sign above them reads, *Welcome back, UC Berkeley Law.*

We approach the table. A woman I don't recognize asks our names, and when I say mine, my eyes light up. "Mack McAllister! Top of our class!"

"Not hardly," I say. "That was Rory. I came in second."

Her cheeks pink up. "Oh, that's right. It was a race to the end."

"We both spoke at graduation," Rory says. "It's an easy mistake."

Old Rory would've had her hackles up. But she's chilled out in the six months since our Christmas revelations. It helps to be at a firm that appreciates her.

I accept my packet. Rory pins my badge on me.

"Rory Sheffield," the woman says, passing Rory her items. "I remember now."

"Thank you. And you are?"

"Amanda Martin. Amanda Jones then."

"Nice to see you, Amanda," Rory says.

"You ready to return to the scene of the crime?" I ask Rory.

She laughs. "Too late to back out now."

As we walk away from the table, I whisper, "I'm sure there's a broom closet here somewhere we could avail ourselves of instead."

Rory grins. "Oh, I plan to do that. We can revisit all our old haunts."

I squeeze her hand. "I like the sound of that."

We enter the big room filled with round tables. We check our packets and find our table number.

When we get there, several packets fill the other spaces.

"I wonder who we're sitting with," Rory says.

"It better be the people I told the committee I wanted to sit with," I say. "I may have pulled a string or two as soon as we committed to coming."

A squeal comes from behind us, and I turn to see Jenessa running toward us. "Mack Squared! Rory! I hear we have Mackory back!"

I accept her quick hug, and she moves on to Rory.

"I've forgotten how tall you are," Rory says.

It's true. Jenessa is five-ten easy, and she's wearing killer heels. In her white sundress with giant red roses, she commands the room.

"This is the point where I bore you with baby pictures," Jenessa says, flipping her phone to face us. "You two are off social media, so you can't say you've seen them already."

She clicks through image after image of her baby. Rory and I stand close together, fingers intertwined. Baby pictures are part of the deal.

There's another squeal. Marta rushes up. "Mackory! The gang's all here!"

I hear Henry's voice before I see him. "Can't say that until I'm at the table."

"Henry!" Jenessa squeals. "You're so bald!" She rubs his head. "What happened to your hair?"

"It all fell out when I had kids."

Jenessa nods knowingly. "Totally get that. Totally. How old are yours?"

"Four and seven," Henry says. He turns to me. "I

miss having you around in Los Angeles, Mack. We can't do our monthly game time."

"I need to fly down for one of those now and then." I shake his hand. It feels good to have everyone together.

Henry sets his packet down next to ours.

"You're assigned to our table!" Jenessa says. "This is going be the best reunion!"

We sit down, Henry showing pictures of his kids to Jenessa, and Marta peppering Rory with questions about her firm in New York.

Jenessa put a pause on her career for her kid, and Marta works in the District Attorney's Office in Atlanta. We've all done perfectly well. I'm glad to see our friends so happy and settled.

"Who else is at our table?" Jenessa asks. She picks up the other packet. "Oh my God, y'all! Oh my God!" Her eyes grow big.

"What is it?" Marta asks.

She lifts the packet to show the name. "It's Saul!" She drops the packet and stands up to peer around the room. "Where is he? He obviously checked in!"

This is a surprise, even for me. We all stand up, searching the room.

Then I feel a tap on my shoulder.

I turn around, and there he is, sun-bronzed and wiry, dressed in a plaid shirt over a T-shirt with cargo pants and strappy sandals. It's clear he paid zero attention to the dress code. Or didn't care.

"Saul," I say, shaking his hand. "So good to see you, man."

The others turn and, realizing who it is, smother him with hugs.

Henry hangs back with me. "He made it. The prodigal Saul has returned."

"I don't spend much time stateside," Saul says. "But my baby sister graduated USC last month, so I decided to hang for a bit before I head back."

"Where's back?" I ask.

"South Africa, right now. We're building legal cases as well as building schools."

"Sit down to tell us all about it," Jenessa says. "We need to catch up."

Saul's eyebrows lift briefly when Rory and I sit close to each other, our hands held on top of the table. But then he grins. "Glad you two finally worked it out. I see I need to get up to speed."

Jenessa waves him off. "Oh, they're old news. Mack became a Santa. Rory couldn't believe it and stalked him. Then they had monkey sex on the Santa sofa in the middle of the damn mall."

Rory sucks in a breath. "Mack! Did you tell them that?"

I don't even get a word out before Jenessa bursts out laughing. "Nope. But now I know. I figured you guys would do that. You two are so crazy."

Rory's face has gone seven shades of pink.

"Oh, don't be like that," Marta says. "It's not like we didn't know the whole time."

"They're in New York," Jenessa tells Saul. "Probably soiling the purity of every subway from Wall Street to Central Park. Henry is in L.A., I'm in San Diego, and

Marta is in Atlanta. Our jobs are boring. Tell us about you."

As Saul regales us with tales of his adventures in the Peace Corps as well as legal aid organizations in far-flung countries, Rory leans her head on my shoulder.

This reunion is the cherry on top of a great summer where we got everything worked out. Rory sold her stake in the Los Angeles firm last January and bought into the partnership in New York. She moved in with her dad while we searched for an apartment on the island.

I split my time between the two coasts until I could get my license in New York squared away and make sure my junior agent was ready for the load. I promoted him, and he took over the clients who absolutely need a Los Angeles-based agent. I've kept my more global clients, the national athletes, and the ones based in other areas. I've also been building my New York roster, which is easy to do with so many great teams concentrated on the East Coast.

Two months ago, we finally found a place to move into. Rory's mom visits a lot more often than we expected, although she prefers to meet us at the Pickle brownstone rather than our own place. I keep telling Rory there's something going on between her biological parents, but she says that's impossible.

Time will tell.

The current dean of the law school taps on the microphone to get our attention, so our conversation has to stop. He's spoken for less than three minutes when Rory elbows me.

She leans in to whisper, "Meet me in the storeroom on the backside of the law library in five minutes."

"You're on."

She slips out of the room, and our friends watch her go.

Saul shakes his head. "And exactly how long until you follow her out so you guys can bang somewhere inappropriate?"

I check my watch, the amazing timepiece Rory put on my wrist on Christmas morning. The engraving, *Our time has come*, rests snugly against my skin on the underside.

"Right about...now."

And I'm off.

EPILOGUE: RORY

I HAVE NEVER SEEN SO MANY SANTAS DRESSED IN FULL regalia in one place. The auditorium of the official Santa School is filled with them.

I pause at the door.

"Isn't it wild?" Mack says.

"It is."

I glance down at my costume. I can't believe I've been talked into this.

I wear a red velvet dress trimmed with fur. The petticoat beneath it makes it stand out a foot away from my body all around. A white fur muff hangs from my wrist by a loop. A curly white wig and red cap make my head look like a pincushion.

But I have to admit, it's cute.

Mack has changed his look this year. He's less traditional Santa, and a bit more of a regal one. Instead of fuzzy, his suit is red velvet interwoven with gold thread. His beard is still straight but much longer, and his mustache is neatly trimmed.

His hair is more subtle, a bit peeking out of his hat and over his ears. He looks like a rather dapper elderly gentleman.

We wander the aisle until we find our seats, oddly in the back corner of the group. I would have thought they would be alphabetical.

The lead Santa instructor can only be described as jolly. He doesn't need a gut pillow. And his beard is his own. He's in full Santa dress, hat, coat, pants, boots. He looks like a Christmas card come to life.

He's one of the most called-upon Santas in the United States, flying across the country for televised appearances, talk shows, and parades. I've had several opportunities to speak with him over the last two weeks while we were in Santa School. He's a person who instantly puts you at ease.

"There is nothing in the world like Santa Claus," he begins, his hands pressed together. "Over the last two weeks, many of you renewed your commitment to spreading the magic of Christmas. Others set out to begin a journey as one of the most beloved figures in history and culture."

He goes on for a bit about traditions, and what will be expected in the coming season. Mack won't be working as a mall Santa this year, but he and I will volunteer for community events and hospitals.

Another Mrs. Claus happens to be seated next to me. She leans over. "He goes on and on. We'll be lucky to be out of here before Christmas."

I try to hide my smile as Santa continues.

"I commend you all for completing your Santa training. From our longest-standing members of the Santa Claus trade to our brand-new recruits, I am delighted to preside over your graduation today."

He turns to his Mrs. Claus, who approaches with a long scroll. "As I call your name, please come to the stage for your certification and diploma."

The parade of Santas and the occasional Mrs. Claus is mesmerizing. The costumes range from the modern traditional red fur to the old-world Father Christmas with gold satin robes.

I imagine there is nothing like this sight in the world.

The procession finally reaches our row. We head to the stairs, watching the Santas ahead of us receive their scrolls.

When we arrive on stage, Santa gives Mack a wink. "Congratulations, Santa and Mrs. Claus. Here are your certifications."

He shakes our hands, but when it's time to walk on, Mack turns around instead.

"Is everything okay?" I ask.

Mack takes my scroll and passes them both back to Head Santa. Then he draws in a big breath. "If you had told me when I was a first-year law student that the driven, studious, outrageously serious Rory Sheffield would ever be on a stage with me dressed as Mrs. Claus, I would never have believed it."

The room rumbles with laughter.

"But one of the great things about being Santa is that you learn to believe. Not just in Christmas and the possibility of miracles, but in yourself. That what you want most in the world can return to you."

I start to understand what he's about to do, and tears prick my eyes. "I've always known that about you," I say.

He nods. "You believing in me is a key part of who we are today." He lifts his hand to reveal a tiny red pouch with fur trim. He opens it and extracts a ring.

Even though I have already guessed what is happening, I still suck in a breath. "Mack?"

He drops to one knee, and all the Santas let out a happy roar of approval.

"Rory Sheffield, would you make me the happiest Santa on earth by becoming my wife?"

When I look at him, I see the Santa he was a year ago when I tried to hide in the line at Riverside Mall and get a glimpse of the man he became while we were apart.

In the last year, I've learned that people can change. They can grow, even if who they are appears to be plenty successful on the outside.

Mack McAllister did something no one else had done. He looked past the person I showed to the world and saw who I really am. He helped me see it, too. And because of that, I've avoided the mistakes of my past, and the ones I learned from my mother. I'm better now. Happier now.

I'm *more*.

I realize I've taken too long to answer, and the auditorium has fallen silent.

I hold out my hand. "Oh my gosh! Yes! Yes!"

"Whew," Mack says. "I thought I was a goner there." He slides the ring on my finger.

Then he stands up and draws me close to him. "Welcome to Santaland, Mrs. Claus," he says.

"This is going to be a Christmas like no other," I tell him.

Just before he kisses me, he says, "Every Christmas from here on out will be the best one yet."

Love the Pickle family? The three brothers each have a love story! Get started with Jason's secret boss romance with Nova in Big Pickle.

AFTERWORD

I wanted to thank all the donor children who have been pushing the issue of anonymous donation to the forefront, particularly in the advent of widespread DNA testing.

For more on the evolving topic of anonymous sperm and egg donation and its impact on children, read several recent articles:

"The Children of Sperm Donors Want to Change the Rules of Conception" by Sarah Zhang. Published in *The Atlantic* October 15, 2021.

"Stop Trying to find the 'Mechanism'" by Rzeka. Published by Medium.com October 7, 2021.

"How a Shortage of Donated Sperm Is Hurting Aussies Who Dream of Being Parents" by Dr. Ryan Rose, PhD. Published on FertilitySA.com.au. on October 7, 2021.

"Couch Genes" a podcast by *Sex, Lies & the Truth*. First broadcast on March 18, 2021.

If your life is impacted by donor conception, visit the Facebook group "Donor Conceived People, Siblings, Parents, and Donors (Sperm, Egg, Embryo)" to connect with others.

BOOKS BY JJ KNIGHT

Romantic Comedies

Big Pickle

Hot Pickle

Spicy Pickle

Tasty Mango

Second Chance Santa

Single Dad on Top

Single Dad Plus One

The Accidental Harem

MMA Fighters

Uncaged Love Series

Fight for Her Series

Reckless Attraction

Get emails or texts from JJ about her new releases:

JJ Knight's list